The SEEING SCROLL

J. T. GROBLER

To Johan
My rock

&

Jocelyn
My light

MAP OF POLYMEAD GROVE
False Bay
Waterfall
Plateau
Oumie's Bench
Bees & Fynbos
Orchards
Vuyo's House
Oupie's Bench
Gia's House
Barn
Factory

Contents

Chapter 1:

Can you keep a secret?

Police exhumed the body in Oupie's coffin, but Gia already knew that it wasn't his.

If only her dad would believe her.

The fingernail wedged between her teeth tore, and she winced as it sliced into her skin. Tears splashed onto her chin, hot, then plopped onto the key she held. It was ancient, solid brass and fat with the promise of secrets. She stroked its back, pondering her hunch about who it came from.

The back door opened.

Gia ducked behind their pepper tree to spy on her dad flicking his long fringe back. Slipping the key into her pocket, she dragged her forearm along her nose, creating yet another snotty streak.

He hopped around and pulled red gumboots over neon-green socks.

A muscle in Gia's jaw twitched. Her plan was underhanded. Sneaky. She'd pay for it if caught, and for a nasty second, she speculated what her punishment would be. She owed it to Oupie, though. Didn't matter what her dad believed.

He whistled for the dogs, but without bothering to wait, plodded from the sprawling, red-brick farmhouse towards the brown-planked barn. Nina, their light-brown Staffordshire terrier who had a broad chest and enormous jaw, charged after him with a gait not quite straight. And Jinja, Gia's red-brown Staffordshire puppy, who wore a rainbow studded collar, followed — hot on everyone's heels. She was as flawless as a puppy could be, Gia thought. The perfect mixture of cocky and cautious.

Polymead Grove cast a gaze across False Bay on the South African coastline. Today, wispy tufts of cloud began where the sloping earth stopped as if they lived on the edge of the world. It ponged of salt, was the kind of place cows outnumbered people, and the single spot on the globe where Gia felt at home. '*We're south of a brick, west of a stick. Just the way I like it.*' Is what Oupie would say.

She lingered until the threesome crossed the cattle-grid which extended across their main gate. It was strange the things she missed, Gia thought. Above all, she longed for the way her dad had laughed while Oupie waddled around. Nowadays, she could have sworn his bulb had blown and replacements weren't available. As much as she wanted to find Oupie for herself, she needed to find Oupie for him. She dared not risk him catching her, though. No doubt he'd suspect she was unravelling faster than a stocking with a hole in. And anyway, it wouldn't be good for him. Nor would a tenth lecture about what she couldn't have seen be fabulous for her. She spot-checked her wristwatch before hobbling towards the house.

One hour and one obstacle remained.

Gia's belly betrayed her. It tightened while she peered at her godfather gobbling down his breakfast at the black granite booth that stretched across the bay-window of their white-wood kitchen. A room with a lingering odour of ground coffee and an odd mixture of antique decor and shiny, modern appliances.

Elias Goodman never lounged against the backrest of anything. He sat as if he'd swallowed a ruler, and his clothes looked as if he'd just folded himself off an ironing board. Plus, his shoes sparkled. They *always* sparkled. Gia didn't need to see or sniff his plate to know what she'd find before him: oats drizzled with raw honey, coffee, no sugar and crispy toast with grated cheddar cheese, crusts cut off. Same as always.

She waited for Elias to open his newspaper. He flapped its pages wide, slapped a dent in the middle with a dark, hefty fist and settled into his ramrod-straight kind of comfy.

A minute passed.

Two.

Judging the moment right, Gia leaned her crutches against the wall, took a deep breath and limped bit by bit across the chessboard floor. Careful not to squeak while putting pressure on her grey-plastic walking brace the doctor called a moonboot, she nicked the key to the study from where it hung beneath the alarm panel. It was the only room in the house they locked. Which was why Gia was convinced it was exactly where Oupie expected her to look.

Elias took a sip of coffee.

Good.

Turning, Gia retrieved her crutches and inched her way across the cavernous living area, passing the piano that had lost its voice since her mom died. She tried to ignore it, but her eyes kept sneaking back without permission. In stealth mode, she slunk along the long corridor, pausing when the redwood floor creaked. Something tap-tap-tapped an angry rhythm and she could have sworn the knotty-pine ceiling groaned.

She stiffened, raked a glance both ways. An African Hoopoe pecked with a vengeance at the horrible bench where Oupie ate his morning eggs. The clouds had disintegrated, False Bay had become visible. And as if it had risen from their ashes, Table Mountain glared at her, bold and steady as an ancient ogre.

An exaggerated clearing of someone's throat pulled Gia's spine straight. The Hoopoe took to the sky with rhythmic, wavelike movements, and she spun just in time to see her best friend skulk into the corridor wearing his trademark, lopsided grin.

'Shh!' she hissed, dripping with guilt.

Vuyo had muscular arms and wide, knobbly knees on bandy legs. He travelled in a bottle-green shirt, pressed jean shorts, sports shoes and an electric blue cap. 'I knew you were up to something. I read about it in my tea leaves.'

'Don't talk rubbish!'

'I can prove it. Wanna know what's happening on Wednesday?'

'Everyone knows you're turning twelve on Wednesday, Vuyo.'

Vuyo rolled his wide-set, long-lashed eyes, but Gia sensed him resisting another grin. He'd swept his raven hair away from his high, honey-coloured forehead with a bone-beaded elastic. The

Arctic opposite of her almost white pixie-cut and blue, apricot-sized blinkers.

'Soooo?' Vuyo leaned his ear in. 'Gonna tell me what you're up to?'

'Depends.'

'On?'

'Can you keep a secret?'

He clicked his tongue. 'I'm already keeping one.'

No less than she'd expected. He hadn't spilt the beans about her mom's bracelet, which she'd lost — the one that used to belong to her grandmother. That and his not-so-humble brag gave him a wee bit of credit. She tugged up her sleeve and checked the time. 'We've got half-an-hour.'

'For what?'

'To search through Oupie's study.'

'They'll ground us till we're wrinkled!'

'Not if you keep watch.'

'So I can be your fall guy?' Vuyo gave an indignant croak.

Gia lifted the key as if she'd won a trophy because he wouldn't be able to resist. Not him.

'Where did you get it?' Vuyo snatched it from her grasp.

'Snail mail.'

'From?'

'No name, no return address either.'

Vuyo opened his mouth, closed it, and made a point of catching her eye. 'Why?'

'Why what?'

'Why assume it has something to do with Oupie?'

Should she tell him? Gia's fist clenched. What if he thought she was batty? What if she was batty? She scanned the yard for her dad. From where she stood, she could make out the white-washed walls and green pitched roof of Vuyo's house, and beyond it, feint signs of a puffing chimney which was the Polymead Grove factory. It's where they made a range of products from propolis. Which was basically bee poo mixed with wax and other gooey stuff. The other sign of civilisation was a russet road. It crossed the bridge where Oupie had rolled his car, then meandered through a valley separated from fields by a patchwork of white picket fences. Smaller paths branched away from it, all going left. A single path swung right and wormed its way down a steep incline, ending at a river nestling in the shade of a mountain which then dribbled its way along the coast. That side of their entire property bordered the sea.

'The car wasn't in the gorge.' Gia risked trusting him because he'd never let her down before.

Vuyo's forehead creased. 'What do you mean?'

She nibbled her thumbnail. 'We stopped rolling on the bridge. The car lay on its roof and it wasn't on fire either, Vuyo.'

His eyelid twitched. He prised her hand away from her mouth but didn't shy from her gaze. 'But your dad said-'

'That Oupie's gone to be with my mother. And life will go on even if it feels like it won't.'

'Ah.' A spark of Vuyo's understanding flashed. He sighed. 'Okay, but... then... how did Oupie's car get into the gorge? Are you saying someone set it alight? That fire's the reason the police exhumed Oupie's coffin, Gia.'

'Nah-uh.' Gia shook her head. 'They've known about the fire from the start, so the police must have learned something new between now and then.'

'Like what?'

'All I know is that if Oupie wasn't in the car, it couldn't have been his body they pulled from the gorge.'

'Whose body was it, then? People don't just appear.'

Her fist clenched and unclenched. 'They don't disappear, either, Vuyo! Oupie's got to be somewhere, right?'

'Waaaiiit a minute.' Vuyo's eyes narrowed. 'Who said Oupie wasn't in the car?'

Gia flicked an imaginary speck of dust from her shoulder, careful to avoid eye contact.

'Tell me!'

'I thought I saw...' Gia's voice cracked. 'Oupie pulled me from the wreckage and put me on the bridge, Vuyo. I wasn't flung. I lapsed into a coma *after* that.' They'd celebrated Oupie's birthday last week Friday, gone for ice cream on Saturday, and she'd woken up in hospital on Tuesday.

Vuyo stared at her with such a listening face. 'Just… don't get your hopes up, that's all I'm saying. Because if you don't know how the car ended in the gorge, then you're missing some fragments, Gia.'

The knot in Gia's stomach unwound a bit when she realised he hadn't rejected her statements outright. 'This key was posted after the accident. My gut says we'll find the answer in there.' She cocked a thumb towards Oupie's study.

'Funny, my gut says we'll find nothing but trouble.'

'Please will you help me? I'll take all the blame if something goes wrong. I promise. You don't even have to come in. Just… cough if someone comes close.'

Vuyo shot her his look of daggers.

It took all her willpower not to smile. She loved the way Vuyo wasn't treating her as if she was glass that would shatter. She'd had more than enough of the 'Oupie-wouldn't-have-wanted' brigade. As if they could read a dead man's — make that a missing man's — mind.

'There must be a reason Oupie's hiding. What if he's in some kind of danger? What if he needs our help? What if-'

'Okay! Geez!' Vuyo lifted his hands in a mock gesture of surrender. 'But five minutes, that's all.'

Gia unlocked the study door and tiptoed across the threshold, closing it just enough to leave a fraction of a lookout gap. Her feet sank into the carpet and she took a moment to relish the fluffy sensation of it creeping between her bare toes that poked out from her moonboot. She adored the study for the same reason she despised it. It oozed Oupie's absence but was drenched by his presence because it reeked of musty tobacco and he'd crammed nautical ornaments into every nook and cranny. She fought to stifle the familiar pang of sadness.

'Yuk! I hate the smell of tobacco.' Vuyo scrunched his nose into a corkscrew and shoved an eyeball in between the door and its post.

Gia hobbled round a nut-brown leather couch with red, chequered, pot-belly cushions and tiptoed towards a gleaming wooden cabinet. She plugged the key into its lock.

Too small.

She shuffled toward Oupie's weapon case. An exhibition of antique guns, knives and mediaeval swords that he'd polished and restored to pristine condition were on display. Not a spec of dust anywhere.

Gia tried the key.

Too big.

Flare guns, maps and a ship's bell lay in the glass display case that stood beside the weapons. Squeezed between them were photographs of her sitting at the piano. Always the piano. Her once-upon-a-time pillar of comfort that had turned against her. There was a large black-and-white picture of Oupie's beaming father, Pop, the founder of Polymead Grove. Wrinkles and furrows of the elderly riddled his face, he had no left ear and a purple scar slanting across his cheek.

She sidled towards the window, scuffled in behind Oupie's desk, and leaned her wooden crutches against a case of antique toy cars that Oupie bought and sold. His hobby of sorts. Gia thrust the key into the long, thin drawer that reached across the desk's middle.

Too long.

She tugged the drawer's handle in frustration. It creaked and popped open.

Fat lot of good it did. The drawer was empty.

Vuyo abandoned his lookout post and sprinted to examine the scene. 'Why would Oupie send you a key that opens nothing?'

'So you do think it came from Oupie?'

'Just hurry up.' He trudged back to his post.

Gia studied Oupie's handsome, seventeenth-century writing desk. A maroon leather inlay covered its top. It had stacks of drawers on either side. Gia rifled through them and found a magnifying glass, rusty pocket-watch, a small pair of binoculars and a long brass telescope. No papers!

She strained to think outside of the box. Oupie was a maverick, after all. Plus, he knew she was twelve, so the answer wouldn't be child's play. Dropping to her knees, Gia shooed a daddy-long-legs across the carpet before crawling under the desk. A bright red alarm button caught her eye. Careful not to touch it, in case it summoned the cavalry, she flipped onto her back and began tapping the panels, checking for hollows. Some had swelled as if swamped by water once.

She leaned her ear against the desk, rapped the panels again. A dull click. Something rolled.

'What's it? What did you find?' Vuyo cantered around the desk and crouched onto his haunches, hovering his head beside hers.

'Shh!'

A swivelling horse-shoe compartment cracked out of the desk in the bottom left-hand corner where Oupie's feet would have been while he sat. Inside it, Gia found a yellow metal tube the length of her palm, no fatter than a drinking straw and sealed with a screw-on lid.

She sat up, unscrewed it and tapped the opening against her palm. Out slid a streaky parchment drizzled with flaky powder and rolled into the shape of a scroll. No markings. Gia dabbed the powder, touched the tip of her tongue. Chalk.

'Open it,' Vuyo commanded.

She peeled the scroll as cautiously as she'd peel an onion, and with the same effect — her vision went blurry. A wave of something powerful blazed through her. An odd whirring noise came from everywhere and nowhere. Oupie's desk trembled and shook. The room spun, once, twice, before the floor gave and they tumbled down a flight of steps, landing headfirst in a dungeon filled with toys.

Swish, swoosh, swish.

A glinting blade spun through the air. Vuyo thrust her sideways as it skimmed their heads.

In the darkness behind them, somebody yelped.

Chapter 2:

When your shadow grows tall

Gia fumbled, fumbled and lost grip of the scroll. With a burst of light, Oupie's study re-emerged and her body shivered from a hand-in-the-freezer sensation. She jerked round, half-and-half expecting to find a knife or a person. Instead, she eyed the scroll curling itself closed.

Vuyo's startled gaze flitted towards her. He pulled up his jaw. 'Tell me you saw that.'

'Was it a proper place? A vision? Illusion?'

'Who screamed? Did you see anyone? Someone must have thrown the knife, Gia.'

'I only saw the knife,' Gia squeaked with a shaky voice before forcing herself to take a calming breath.

Vuyo swept up strands of his silky smooth hair that had come loose. He retied his ponytail with his beaded elastic before edging forward to hunch over the scroll with simmering curiosity. 'It came from this.'

'It felt like… magic.'

'I have no idea how magic feels, but that thing's dangerous!' His eyes shone as if he'd hit upon a marvellous opportunity.

Gia crept closer. The scroll hadn't changed. *How very odd.* 'What was that place? *Where* was it? Were we transported into that dungeon, do you think? Or did it pop up around us?'

Vuyo reached out.

'Don't!' She elbowed him in the ribs before he did something they'd both regret. 'What if we end up back there?' She could have sworn Vuyo looked even more enchanted. *Boys!* Gia tried to breathe. Putting the metal tube in line with the roll of parchment, she used the tube's lid and slid the scroll back into its casing.

Where on earth did Oupie, *her* Oupie, get something magical from? Nothing could be further from what she'd been expecting.

'What do you want to do, then? Stick it back where we found it?'

'Huh-uh! Oupie wanted us to find it for a reason!' Gia inspected her crutches. She picked the one she'd marked with a teeny-tiny dot of pink nail polish and yanked loose the dense, spongy bit - the piece which slotted underneath her armpits. She crammed the scroll into the crack above her unasked-for stash of pain pills, certain it made a cosy temporary hiding place. 'Let's keep it with us until we figure out why Oupie wanted us to have it.'

She zipped one last glance across the study, making sure nothing was disturbed, lest Elias spot a strand of hair which hadn't been there before. They shut the study door and crept back down the passage.

'Can I have a go?' Vuyo took her crutches once they'd reached the family room. He hopped away as if the devil chased him.

Gia passed a row of photographs. They crafted an album of her life: Oupie and her dad wearing black-tie, Vuyo baking mud cakes and her mom bridling her horse, Lipica. The white Lipizzaner mare who'd changed their lives so dramatically. Gia tried quelling the memory of white rose petals strewn across the piano, hundreds of candles being lit and her dad's glazed-eye expression while he stood beside her with a hand on her shoulder, helping her absorb the barrage of sorrowful whispers. She huffed, annoyed with herself for lapsing into a day better left forgotten. Was it so terrible, though, to wish things could go back to being the way they once were?

Elias had gone. His spot cleared, so Vuyo slid into the granite booth.

Gia opened the fridge and poured two glasses of fresh orange juice. She fetched a bowl of chocolate-chip cookies and slid into the booth opposite him. She handed him the key. He got busy assessing it from tip-to-toe, head bent in concentration.

The bay-window booth was Gia's second favourite spot in the house. It had a way of bringing the countryside indoors, boasting an outstanding view of faraway cliffs and tiny ships crossing a wind smacked sea. Her gaze drifted towards their never-ending Pink Lady apple orchard. On spring days like today when the air was zippy and the sky, clearer than a brand new page, it swarmed with fluttering white butterflies. Alongside the orchard was a firebreak and a small orange grove. To the right of their road, because Oupie was an apiarist, stretched acres and acres of *fynbos* crammed with boxed beehives. She smiled at the idea of the pesky little creatures, but stiffened when she caught sight of Lipica grazing in her paddock.

Vuyo chomped a biscuit, leaning over the plate to catch the crumbs. 'Maybe it-' He drew the key to his chest and, pulling a face, twisted each end in opposite directions.

Nothing happened.

He rolled his dark, dreamy eyes and twisted his hands the other way. The ridge along the stem of the key swivelled and a mischievous grin festered on his cheeks. He barked out a proud laugh and made a ta-da gesture before holding it over the table and tugging its handle and stem in different directions. Out dropped a rolled-up note. It looked different from the scroll. It wasn't old, for one thing.

Gia scooped up the note, ironing it open with her palm. 'There's something written on it! Listen.

'Those who know thereof do not speak.

Those who speak cannot know.'

'Sounds like a warning.' Vuyo whistled on intake of his breath causing Gia to clench her toes. 'Oupie wants us to keep this secret.'

'There's writing on the back, too.' She squinted at the tiny words. 'It's a riddle!'

'I don't speak riddle.'

'Listen!' She read it aloud.

'When your shadow grows tall,

enter beneath the bent wall.

Follow the path to the end,

find the place where fate began its trend.'

Gia's cheeks cracked into a grin. It was as if Oupie was right beside her suddenly, egging her on in his weird and huggable way. 'It's definitely from Oupie, Vuyo! He knew we'd be eager to tackle this. It might lead us to what the key's for.'

'Treasure?' Vuyo's eyes sparkled.

'To where he's hiding, you muppet.'

'Did he leave a map?'

'He left a riddle.'

'He should have left a map.' Vuyo closed an eye, peeping the other into the key's stem.

'A riddle is a map… It's a map for smart people.'

'Where we gonna find one of those?'

'Oh, come on! It's not as if Oupie was a rocket scientist.'

Vuyo looked doubtful.

'If you help me and we find treasure, I'll split it with you. Eighty, twenty. What do you say?' Gia held up her thumbs.

'Dream on.'

'Just kidding. Fifty, fifty,' she giggled, dangling the carrot.

Vuyo spat on his palm and held it towards her because nothing said promise to a boy quite like a handful of gob. 'Okay, let's see.' He pulled his mouth to the side and chewed the inside of his cheek. '*When your shadow grows tall*. Shadows stretch in the mornings and afternoons.'

'So… Oupie doesn't want us searching for him at night?'

'Exactly.'

'See? Easy-peasy.'

'*Enter beneath the bent wall.*'

'What about that?' Gia pointed through the window, allowing her eyes to trace the wall of white stone encircling their yard. It wasn't high, four feet perhaps, but thick as a prison wall and after sending her thoughts through the garden of ideas they come back pondering why. It defended nothing other than freshly mowed grass and cheerful flower beds.

Vuyo gave a disapproving grunt. 'Going beneath that kind of wall would take us underground.'

'Unless… the riddle's referring to a wall that's in the air?'

'A bridge or an archway?'

Gia nodded, struggling to mask her disappointment. There was a pickle. The single arch in the air that she knew of was the bridge where Oupie's car had rolled. Why would he hide anything there?

'What about the service roads by the river? Oupie's almost the only person who used them. There are strangely shaped rocks down there, maybe one of them has an arch?'

'Brilliant!' She punched him playfully in the chest.

'I'll zip down there. Check on our half-baked theory.'

'What?' Gia's heart snagged. 'You can't go without me.'

'But...' Vuyo wrinkled his nose and gestured at the oh-so-inflexible contraption on her foot.

Gia furrowed her forehead, thought for a minute, then smiled a cat smile. 'Don't worry. I have an idea.'

'Oh, boy,' Vuyo breathed.

Chapter 3:

Suspect number one

Vuyo dummied left, crab crawled right, scuttling to get a decent view of a storeroom that Gia thought, ponged of mildew and wet box. 'Hey, do you think your dad will mind if I bang about on his bike?' Vuyo pointed.

'Of course not. But don't you prefer yours?'

'It's in the river.' He pulled up his shoulders. 'Don't ask,' he slurred, lowering a blue mountain-bike from the wall and wheeling it to the door before darting back and searching between packages. Dipping, he vanished behind a box and reappeared holding a kind of skateboard with wheels no bigger than a pair of adult fists, and covered in traction. Positioned at the skateboard's rear was an engine with a small petrol container.

The last gift her mom had given her.

Vuyo pulled the purple handlebar which folded into the skateboard base, it clicked into place and a go-ped took form. 'Okay, let me see.' He fiddled with its gadgets a little. 'This is the start button, these are the brakes, and that's the accelerator. Did I mention these are the brakes?' He winked.

Gia rolled her eyes, pretending she needed to be told twice.

'Go on, then. Give it a bash.'

The go-ped wobbled and wobbled, but Gia had no doubt the strength of her grip was amazing.

'Give it more gas!' Vuyo hollered.

'Why?'

'Try!'

Weirdly, when she pulled the accelerator a tad more, the go-ped steadied and her quivering circle grew steadier by the minute.

Vuyo whoop-whooped and punched the air. 'Now practise while I fix up the bike!'

Gia's eyes watered from rushing air. She scrunched them into slits, blinking to refocus. The go-ped's wheels hit the round, metal bars of the cattle-grid creating an up-down, up-down sensation making her teeth chatter. She released the throttle out of pure panic and the scooter free-wheeled to a shaky halt. But suddenly, she got it: the terror surging through her, the exhilaration of speed and grits of earthy filth sticking to her face made her thrilled to be alive!

She yanked the accelerator this time, scooting past the split-pole structure of Lipica's paddock. At the vegetable patch, she swung a snug circle and turned back towards the house, suffering through a gagging stench of cow dung. The creatures watched her while lazying about in the sweltering sun, their bottom jaws moving in that strange circular motion.

In the yard, Vuyo slapped her a high-five and flashed her an admiring grin. 'Told you, you'd be able to do it.'

'It's nice to see you out and about again, Gia.' Elias' monotonous-as-a-clock voice twanged.

Catching a whiff of peppermint, Gia spun around. Elias moved closer. Of everyone she knew, he had the strangest way of speaking. His mouth seldom moved. It was as if his tongue had grown lazy and he manufactured words in the space behind his teeth.

'How are you feeling?' His face softened.

'Good, thanks.' Gia craned her neck back to look at his face.

Elias ruffled her hair and gave a thin-lipped smile. 'And the foot?'

She lifted her moonboot, showing him it's comfy foam lining and how it tightened behind her calf with adjustable Velcro strips.

'Is that what you were looking for?' Elias pointed at the go-ped.

Gia nodded.

'Perhaps… wear your helmet?'

'I won't go fast.'

Elias rolled his head and flicked his chin towards the barn.

Gia peered around him, caught sight of her dad and felt a horrid little kick in her stomach.

Her dad must have sensed them watching him somehow, because he looked up, stopped prodding a cow's stomach, and waved. 'Hey, Sweetheart! Great day, isn't it?' he hollered, his fringe slapping his face.

Gia waved back. She adored his smile and hated the thought of him not doing it again. Especially because of her insensitivity. 'I'll find it,' Gia mused, looking Elias in the eye.

He squeezed her shoulder, dipped his dark head and glared at Vuyo with an expression that remained unchanged. 'What about you, Son? Did you find what you were searching for in the study?'

Drat! Gia's cheeks got hot and surely red. She swallowed and fought to keep a straight face.

Neither of them said anything. It would tank them.

Vuyo's head hung lower and Gia marvelled, not for the first time, at how different he was from his father. Air thick with silence, Vuyo threw her his kill-me-now admission of guilt while Elias continued in his same-old-same-old tone.

'Every good sleuth knows that alarm panels have zones and zone lights flash where there's movement.' He gazed at Gia with a peculiar intensity.

Gia sensed warmth spread up her neck. Why point out where they'd gone wrong? Was he expecting them to continue snooping? Fun fact — if Oupie was a cat, Elias would be his ball of yarn. Despite their age difference, they were brothers in a certain way and inseparable. Elias had come to Polymead Grove at the age of six after his dad had upped and left and his mother, Bongi, had given up her job as a fortune teller when she was forced to fend for him. Bongi and Pop were thick as thieves. Together, they'd developed the creams and lotions made in the Polymead factory. *'No small feat,'* Oupie had said, because selling bee products had saved them from collapsing into debt. These days, though, Elias and Oupie were business partners with fifty-fifty shares of the Polymead Grove factory. Elias ran the bee-product side of the factory, while Oupie focused on manufacturing honey mead, and Bongi did the quality control. But she'd read your palm if you dared to dare her. And she was the best story-teller this side of the stars. Gia had been charmed on many a sleepover with tales of mythical creatures, legends of faraway lands, and the horrors of artefacts better left forgotten. How Bongi had produced a son so solemn of manner, not even a fairy could guess. Oupie said it was because Elias had spent his childhood trying to be perfect. He'd hoped it would make his dad come back to them. To this day nobody had the foggiest what became of his father. Gia's heart ached for him. Losing a parent was hard to accept, even when you knew where they'd gone.

Aside from her, only Elias was named in Oupie's Will. And for some oddball reason that no sane person could fathom, Oupie had left him beehive numbers four, eight and twenty from his personal collection. It struck Gia as strange suddenly. Why had Oupie given him something he already had plenty of? What if the numbers were a code? Then again, why would Oupie give Elias a code but send her the key? Unless… the numbers had been meant for her ears? As the beneficiary of Oupie's estate, he would have known she'd be present at the reading of his Last Will and Testament. Was it possible that those hives contained clues? It seemed a great place for secrets. How on earth would she raid a beehive without getting stung? Another fun fact — the person with the skill to do just that was standing right in front of her. Gia narrowed her eyes. Labelled her godfather suspect number one.

Vuyo cleared his throat and tried pushing the go-ped around his dad.

'If your mother catches you rifling through Oupie's stuff, Kiddo, she'll boil you like a frog.'

Vuyo gave a quick laugh of terror at the idea of Tammy. 'I didn't… I wasn't-'

'Good. Because I won't be saving any frogs. Consider yourself warned,' Elias murmured, spun on his shiny shoes and strode away.

Chapter 4:

Beneath the bent wall

Gia tossed and turned, checked and re-checked her watch. Did Oupie want her to bring the scroll to him? Was that what the key and the riddle was for? Her body tingled with excitement at the prospect of seeing him again. A key, a secret horse-shoe compartment, a dungeon, a riddle, *a warning*, numbers for hives — it was all so marvellous.

She flat-slapped her hands over her nose and mouth, cringing from shame. How could she be so single-minded? Her heart ached for the man found in their gorge. Where had he come from? And why? Who was he? He wasn't in Oupie's car when it rolled — fact! What would happen when police realised that it wasn't Oupie in the morgue? How would her dad react?

What about his family? Were they searching for him too? A dry popcorn sensation crawled into her throat, and she worried she might puke when the darkest of thoughts crossed her mind. What if he was somebody's dad?

She propped herself against her headboard, crossed her arms and tried to suppress the shivers rippling through her body. The gaping question. How on earth did Oupie's car get into the gorge? She'd have to fish around in the morning, find out what her dad…

Gia didn't realise she'd fallen asleep until the back door banged, a sniff of melting butter and crispy toast floated through the crack beneath her bedroom door and sprinklers started hissing like cats. She rubbed her eyes with her knuckles, stretched, threw together an outfit and hobbled into the kitchen. The helmet she'd found was on the table, red with purple blots. The go-ped and her dad's bike were on the porch. Gia peered through the window and groaned at the slice of slanting sunlight that appeared to be competing with sulking rain clouds. She'd loathe to write off another day.

Slicing a peach, Gia knelt and crawled under the booth that stretched across their bay-window. She fed it to the tortoise who sometimes meandered into the house. The dot of shocking orange nail polish she'd branded him with was how she recognised it was the same one. And how she kept track of its growth. Somebody had to.

Her dad's gumboots materialised like little red ghosts from beyond. He stamped a puddle of mud from their soles at the back door, unpeeled his feet and padded across the kitchen in canary-yellow socks. Gia listened to him scrub his hands before popping the kettle switch.

Nina didn't bother cleaning her paws, she strolled mud across the floor. Jinja proudly did the same. She spotted Gia under the table and stormed across the kitchen, trying her best to sit on the exact spot Gia occupied. Gia gurgled with pleasure. In her view, nothing spelt puppy as much as a warm fat paunch, spiky teeth, foul breath and a tail that travelled at twice the speed of light. And when she told Jinja her darkest worries, she kept it to herself. Every time.

'What are you doing under the table?' Her dad's socks turned towards her.

'Feeding Speedbump.'

'You didn't pick him up, did you?'

'No!'

'Good. Because the water he'd give off isn't pee like some kids say. It's what he's hoarding to help him survive the summer.'

'I remember.' Gia crawled from underneath the booth and Jinja rushed to sniff the reptile's butt as a way of greeting while her dad planted his once-a-day peck onto her forehead. The stench of dung still on his shirt.

Her mother was a hugger; Oupie too, her dad was a secret locked inside himself. He looked exhausted. But after giving her the once-over, his cheeks cracked into a half-moon smile that lit his face like a bulb.

Sometimes it was a bit of a dilemma deciding on which colour to wear, so Gia tried to wear them all. Aside from her moonboot, she wore a sports shoe the colour of a Christmas stocking, a neon-green cap and her favourite skinny jeans — pink in front and tangerine at the back. And to round it off, a sun-shirt with yellow, blue and purple stripes.

'Hey, Mister Lance.' Vuyo ambled in looking swell in a turquoise shirt, black board shorts and black sneakers.

'Gabriel,' her dad corrected.

They shook hands, punched their fists together and shook hands again.

'Gia won't forget about the tortoise. She's planning to follow in your footsteps,' Vuyo murmured.

Her dad's face clouded and his worry lines crinkled.

'And become a vet, I mean,' Vuyo added.

'Ah, so geek-freak is a family trait.' Her dad winked, his face jovial even though his eyes remained sad.

'I'd rather be friends with a geek than an airhead.' Vuyo shrugged.

'Exactly what I'd expect a bookworm to say.' Gia's father grinned again. He stood beside Vuyo to inspect the picnic goodies Gia had gathered for their expedition: lemonade, strawberries, oranges, ham with cheese crackers, chips and strips of liquorice. 'I wonder if that will be enough,' he quipped and punched Vuyo playfully in the gut. The phone rang, and he shuffled to where it hung beside the alarm panel. They listened to his one-sided conversation. But not on purpose.

'Hello, Gabriel Lance. *Yes,* that Gabriel Lance. Oh, hello, Detective.' A frowning forehead pause. 'What kind of hiccup?' He scowled across the kitchen and the moment he noticed them watching him, he turned his back on them.

Something's happened!

'Why not? When will you be able to say?' her dad barked, grouchy now. 'Samuel George Morgan. Of course I'm sure. What else would it be?' He rang, more like banged, off and stomped away, leaving Gia staring at him, bewildered.

In the yard, Gia fastened her helmet. She balanced her crutches on the scooter's base, centred them between her arms, and eased the go-ped a few careful metres forward. Vuyo, riding her dad's bike, sped away, cast her his look-at-me grin, slammed on brakes and threw out the bike's back wheel, skidding up a spiral of dust. *Boys!*

Gia crossed the cattle-grid with the dogs trotting along beside her. She moved past the orange grove and took the road to the river that was lined with red, sweet-smelling roses nestled below stripes of oak trees that were perfect for climbing. Vuyo ramped over speed bumps again and again, and with a face of utter bliss while she kept a firm grip on the brakes, ensuring that she picked tactical paths between ruts. Soon, the road sank so low that the mountains edging the coast obscured their view of False Bay, and a constant *bzzzzzzz* filled the air.

'Hurry!' Vuyo pedalled in the manner of a bandit fleeing a crime scene until he'd out-cycled the boxes of hives lurking between shrubs.

Gia tried stifling her giggle after she found him waiting beneath a clump of trees, beside the earthy mound of an anthill.

Vuyo fluttered his eyelids. 'Bees have a strong sense of community, in case you don't know. In swarms like these, you only need one of them to go mad before they all turn psycho and everything goes to pot.'

A cackle burst from her chest but she couldn't help spying around, all too aware that if just one hive got its knickers in a knot, Vuyo would outrun her and she'd be the dimwit on whom they poked their revenge. She stood for a moment watching a butterfly land on her hand. It wasn't afraid of bees, she realised, then blew softly onto its wings, making it take off.

Gia scrutinised the man-made boxes. It amazed her that bees didn't seem to mind using them as hives. There were tags on the lids, numbers, but obscured by the sheer volume of bees loafing on them. If they wanted to find beehive number four, eight and twenty, no doubt they'd have to come after dark. That was the simple part. Raiding an active hive without getting stung, now *that* was a different matter. She shivered at the prospect. Perhaps she should try to work something out while she lay awake at night.

Minutes later, Gia delighted in the odour emitted by the river, the sound of water gurgling and the raucous chattering of a flock of lemon-yellow Sociable Weavers who clung to nests resembling lightbulbs.

She listened to the crunch of leaves and crackle of twigs under Vuyo's sneakers as he trundled into the rough bits, scouting for walls or secret entrances while she searched the service roads for structures that qualified as an arch. All she encountered was a pump house with a handle that curved upwards in the shape of a dog's tail.

By the time the sun passed the centre of the sky, Gia was sweating streams. Her air of purpose had dwindled and her hair stuck to her head in clumps of dampness — beyond flattering. Her foot throbbed and the toes sticking out of her moonboot looked like bruised bananas, so they stopped to picnic at a house-high waterfall which poured down the edge of the mountain on the coastal side of the river. On the riverbank, tucked beneath a tree, white lilies and bullrushes surrounded a rocky pool. A wooden bench overlooked it. Gia's late Oumie had lounged there for hours watching adventurous ducklings while revelling in soft drizzles of spray that clung to her face.

Warm oranges tasted divine, Gia decided. Jinja enjoyed them too. She licked runaway juice from Gia's chin before working on an escape tunnel which, at first glance, she was digging to England!

'Germs, Gia!' Vuyo moaned. He washed his hands, rinsed his face and put his long feet on top of a rock, skipping stones across the pool while trying, in between, to drown passing leaves with his karate chop. He had a knack for contentment. What bliss, Gia decided. No matter what he did, where he was, he relished the moment.

She snapped thin branches from a shrub, and because it drove her bonkers, experimented with how to reach that annoying itch inside her moonboot. She stuck her foot on a rock, lay on her back and used Nina as her cushion, glad for the rising wind that cooled her. Except for wasps hovering along the edges of the stream imitating miniature flying drones, it seemed the perfect place to breathe and recharge. Gia eyed the weeping willow that had grown up buckled, marvelling at the way small pockets of sky peeped through its leaves.

'Wanna try the bridge?' Vuyo shouted, his voice gobbled up by the rumble of tumbling water.

Gia watched a Fish Eagle circling. A gust of wind whipped through the willow bending its branches like an old man's back and an idea popped into her head quicker than a sneeze. 'Wait a minute. What if we're being too literal?'

Vuyo looked up.

Gia stood in a rush, driven by her idea. 'What if the *bent wall* isn't a solid structure? Look at the branches.' She pointed before inspecting her surroundings further. 'See how the water pushes over the top edge of the waterfall? It's bending, isn't it? Maybe we should search for that kind of thing?'

'Let's look behind it.' Vuyo's eyes shone. 'That would put us *beneath a bent wall*, wouldn't it? Maybe there's a cave. Lots of waterfalls shield hidden caves.'

'Yes! No, wait,' Gia squawked and her stomach lurched.

'I told you you'd regret not being able to swim.' Vuyo smothered a smirk.

Gia glanced around again, desperate now. She gestured at some jagged sun-baked rocks the shade of an elephant's trunk. 'You can help me hop across those. They look like they lead to the waterfall.'

'The water's deep there,' Vuyo snorted.

'Then the rocks are safer than being *in* it!'

'And if the tide rises and covers them while we're busy, what then? Can you imagine me trying to explain to our dads what happened to you? Never mind my mom!'

Gia inspected the rocks again. The water *was* treacherous, but the path looked dead-bone dry. She judged the tide would take hours to come in. Then shot Vuyo a surly gaze, stewing. 'Okay. You better teach me to swim.' She stuck her nose in the air and sprung a fake cheery tone. 'We'll come back next week or the week after that, depending on how long it takes. Assuming I'll even *be* able to swim. Oumie couldn't, you know! So it might not be in my genes.'

Ting. Round one to me! She read the writing on Vuyo's face. The one thing she'd had to seduce him with and she'd found it — time. He'd rather kiss a fish than sit around waiting for her to learn the doggy paddle. His black eyes glared at her before darting towards the path. Gia could have sworn his mind was weighing the odds.

'I suppose my shoes *do* have great traction.'

'I wouldn't suggest it if I didn't think it was safe. You know I'm rubbish at risking my neck.'

'Promise to hold on tight.'

'Promise!'

'I mean it, Gia. No matter what happens, don't let go of me.'

'Pinky swear!' Gia presented him with her little finger, which he took.

Vuyo straddled the rocks in pairs. He put his arms on the sides of her waist and helped her hop from one to the other while Jinja acted like a frog crossing lily pads. Gia peered around the waterfall in no time.

'Do you see anything?' Vuyo screeched.

'A ledge!'

'Climb it!'

Gia's worry bone objected. 'I dunno.'

'Hold on to me.' Vuyo lifted her. He did the same with Jinja before hopping onto the ledge between them.

Gia gritted her teeth and slid with her back against the knobbly mountain as if it was her closest and dearest friend.

'One foot at a time,' Vuyo encouraged.

Gia shuffled sideways, using her crutches to brace: crutch, moonboot, foot, crutch, crutch, moonboot, foot, crutch. Crutch — it got stuck. She yanked and plucked. It gave. The sound she heard next was so loud, she thought the planet had cracked. Gia whipped her head left, right, eyes wide. 'What was that?'

The unthinkable happened.

The mountain grunted.

And then it moved.

'Vuyo?' Gia's mouth went dry.

'Gia!' Vuyo howled, frail as a distant foghorn. He threw out an arm.

Gia's end of the mountain shifted inwards. The end at which Vuyo stood shot out, knocking him towards the river.

'Vuyo!' Gia clawed for his hand, her heart hammered against her ribcage.

Vuyo's scrabbling fingers slipped through hers and he clenched empty air. 'Jump!'

With an ensemble of shrieks, and convinced the door was itching to crush her beneath it, Gia seized her crutches and dived in the direction the rock moved.

Splash! Jinja hit the water.

The last thing Gia saw was Vuyo doing a crazy on the side, eyes urgent and screaming like a banshee before things went as dark as a dungeon.

Chapter 5:

The key

Light dipped like the brief lull of a power surge before daylight resumed a feeble strength. The gruesome echo of stone grinding on stone came to an abrupt halt. Goosebumps trickled up her arms. She tasted blood and even though the breeze following her in freshened stale air in pockets, a dead-rat pong assaulted her nostrils.

Gia stayed still. Listened hard. Aside from her panting breath, the place was silent as a tomb. Where was she? Could it be the dungeon they'd seen through the scroll? Waiting for her eyes to adjust was torture. What if she wasn't safe here?

A quick inspection of her surroundings confirmed that she'd been sealed into a cave that was home to nothing but a few lone rocks. One end was so black it looked like the place where darkness was invented. A frail patch of light trickled in from the opposite side. It spilled at an angle across a flight of man-made, red-brick steps which curled around a column.

Were there people there? Oupie maybe? It seemed a good place to hide. Gia clenched her fists and swung for the wall. No time for that now! She had to get back to Vuyo. His scream burrowed into her brain and she cursed her haste. Ants had better judgement. What if he'd bumped his head on a rock? Or fallen into the river? What about Jinja? Just because she hadn't tried swimming, did it mean she couldn't? Her dad said that not all dogs could swim! Gia pictured her puppy sinking into the river.

Think... think... think. Get. Yourself. Under. Control.

She wiped foul mud from her lips and rubbed grit from her fingertips onto her knees, then glared at the wall and concentrated on concentrating. It didn't matter if the door wasn't visible; it was there, and doors opened from both sides. So — there had to be a mechanism similar to the one on the other side. It must be what her crutch had caught on. She had to find it!

Gia examined the ground and crawled along, retracing her footprints and the great gouges ripped into the mud by her clawing fingers. She'd gone a few paces before she threw the back of her hand over her mouth, swallowing a gasp.

Was that a boot print?

She peered harder. It was large. A strange smell chipped away at the stale air. There, then not, then there again. Peppermint? Gia lifted her nose, sniffed. Never had time to decide.

The mountain groaned.

A fracture appeared in the rock-face. She watched in awe as an arch-shaped mountain door rotated at a central point. Equal sides swung in tandem. For a split-second, she glimpsed the waterfall and heard its rushing voice before Vuyo sprang through, karate chop at the ready. The muscles in his jaw flexed and his expression of dread back-peddled into a half-moon smile filled with such hard-to-miss relief that Gia grinned back. Her shoulders slumped, and she heaved a breath.

'Told you there was a cave!' Vuyo mumbled matter-of-factly. He dusted his shirt with precision and folded away his fists by placing his hands on his hips and peering down his nose at her. 'I figured out how the door works,' he slurred, making no effort at all to hide his smirk before proceeding to take a bow of thanks from an imaginary audience.

'Jinja?'

'She's fine. Heart of a tiger, that one. Swims like one too.'

'You're lucky you didn't bump your head,' Gia quipped.

'I bumped my elbow.' Vuyo dangled a wide gash in her face.

Boys! Here she was, practically planning his funeral, and all he did was brag about a scratch as if he'd won a medallion. He didn't need to know how worried she'd been, she decided.

Vuyo twisted towards the patch of light. 'That must be the *follow the path to the end* bit of the riddle.' He tugged Gia to her feet and fetched her crutches before moving towards the steps. 'Let's check it out.'

Gia eyed the ground. Vuyo's footsteps had muddied everything. She sniffed. The air seemed fresher now, with a slight tang of the ocean. Was it a boot print she'd seen, though? Or had her imagination been playing tricks?

Vuyo's wristwatch beeped.

'Ag, man.' He glanced at his wristwatch and punched the air aggressively. The dials had turned neon-green because of the dark. 'Just when we were getting somewhere.'

'What? What are you talking about?'

'I have to milk the cows today. That's my reminder. Afterwards, I have to clean the porch because you guys are coming for dinner.'

Cows were milked twice a day. Between Gia's dad and Elias, they shared a rotating schedule. But during school holidays, Vuyo plucked on their udders in the afternoons. They used the milk at the Polymead Grove factory, some in the house, and excess was delivered to the nearest village. Tammy had arranged for a small refrigeration truck to collect the leftovers every afternoon.

'My dad already thinks we're up to something, Gia. If we're late, it will confirm his suspicion. And if I don't pitch, he'll mention it to *your* dad, who'll mention it to *my* mom. We can both guess how that ends!'

'She'll plan the rest of our holiday — more like dictate it down to the minute.'

'Exactly!'

Gia stared at the flight of steps, and her heart filled with longing. She'd been counting on finding Oupie today.

'We better not push my mom's buttons, Gia.'

Vuyo was right. Of course he was. They wouldn't be able to find Oupie or help him if Tammy locked them in the house. She wouldn't put it past Tammy to cancel their holiday, either. Because they were homeschooled and Tammy was their teacher. Gia hadn't always been. Four months had passed since she'd dragged a classmate around by the roots of her hair when the girl had the gall to joke about Gia's mom not being able to keep her balance on a horse. And it hadn't been an accidental miss-speak!

'Definitely not. No! My Gia will most certainly not be apologising,' Oupie informed the principal while fetching her from the quarantine corner they'd stored her in. A place kids only escaped with parental guidance. And he'd accepted her side of the story without flinching. *'And Gabriel won't help raise money for your music department! Not after this!'* he'd yelled, thrown in an explosion of curses, and banged the door so hard even the windows had shuddered from fright. Gia was willing to bet that the principal had never met a man with such a foul mouth and loony-bin temper.

Elias said there was no shame in missing a loved one. Bongi said she didn't have to apologise for defending the dead. The principal should have known better. Tammy said that just because having a mother wasn't part of her story anymore, didn't mean kids should throw it in her face like that. She'd phoned the girl's mother and paid them a visit. It ended in a shouting match which Tammy won, hands down. Gia's dad… never said a word. He'd stared at her with his long face of hopelessness and nodded in agreement when Oupie suggested homeschooling might be better for everyone. At least for a while. If only her dad believed in her the way Oupie did.

Gia quashed her thoughts, eyeing the steps again. Oupie felt so close and yet so far. 'Can we take five minutes to see what's here?' She jabbed a finger at the steps. 'To the top and back?'

'Only if I don't have to wait for you once we get back across the river?' Vuyo bartered, even though it was obvious he was as eager as she was.

'Deal! But I keep the dogs.'

'Deal!'

They climbed a short flight of steps and came upon an archway built from dark wood and blocked by a sturdy gate with thick metal bars littered with rust spots. Something you'd expect to find in a castle's dungeon. Gia ran her fingers over a snarling dragon head on the gate's handle and something stirred in her memory. 'Does this seem familiar to you?'

'Mmm, maybe.' Vuyo pursed his lips. 'This kind of gate must be guarding heaps of treasure!' He beamed but fell into a pout as if he'd swallowed a mouthful of sour grapes. 'I hope it's keeping us from going in and not stopping some psycho dude from coming out.'

Gia didn't fancy that idea. Not one bit. She craned her neck, trying to get a glimpse of what lay beyond. More stairs? Wouldn't that lead to the mountain that bridged the gap between their farm and the sea? She leaned in, caught the occasional gurgle of running water, nothing more. For a second, she considered calling Oupie's name to see if he came. But her gut warned her. The gate was old. It appeared to have been there since the dawn of time and Oupie had only been missing for a week. So who had built it? Why? What did it have to do with Oupie's disappearance? How did the scroll fit into things? One thing was certain — there was no doubt in her mind. She was exactly where Oupie wanted her to be.

And the gate was the reason he'd sent her the key.

Chapter 6:

Those who know thereof

Gia stepped gingerly around the Grand piano.

For the longest time, the instrument had been her favourite spot in the house and wielded a kind of mystical attraction over her. Now it tortured her with her happiest memories and her worst. She couldn't get away from it. She skimmed her fingertips along the delicate, flowery inlays on its lid and risked opening the keyboard. Laying her palm flat, Gia closed her eyes, inhaled and slid it slowly across the cool, white keys before shifting it back again. She wasn't sure how long it had engrossed her before she realised her dad was leaning against the half-wall behind her, in his purple and orange socks.

Gia snapped her hand away and spun to face him.

He chomped the last bite of his toast, licked his lips, downed his coffee and strolled across the room delivering his kiss-of-the-day before closing the piano.

Limping closer to the window, Gia dug her hands into her shorts, admiring the spring day with sweltering heat the world had gifted them. That's when she heard it. Faint at first, but distinctly different from the vibrations of a farm. Her nose wrinkled as she watched a sea of twirling blue lights snake towards the house, red dust ballooning in their wake. The sounds of their engines grew gruffer and gruffer as the vehicles raced closer and closer. Gia's jaw practically dropped onto her sleeve.

They must have finished the autopsy!

She backed against her dad, slipped her palm into his. 'You don't have to worry, Daddy. It will be okay. You'll see.' If anything, he looked more troubled, so she gave his hand her firmest reassuring squeeze. At least they knew what the drama was about. Forewarned meant forearmed, wasn't that the saying? Gia swallowed and tried with all her might to ignore the chilling thrill of nerves tightening her chest.

Five patrol cars flew across the bridge and skidded to a halt in the driveway. A police officer hopped from the leading sedan and rapped on the windows, waving a search warrant as if preparing for combat.

A tall, big-boned man with brown, bloodshot eyes, who bulged in the middle like a Russian Nesting Doll took his time strolling across the threshold. Detective Harrison Steele moved from room to room, poking this and, prodding that, acting as if everything in their house was interesting or suspicious. His voice boomed, making it clear who led the investigation. Not to mention that everyone called him Sir. He ordered them to lock the dogs in the storeroom because Nina growled at a policewoman which, Gia thought, should have told Detective Steele exactly what he needed to know about her character.

A nagging sense that she struggled to quash jogged through her belly. She watched in silence while police rummaged through her crowded bookshelf, pulling clothes from her drawers. A police officer even put a hand between Gia's mattress and base, feeling her way around it. Gia realised she wouldn't need a grownup to confirm that they weren't searching for Oupie. What *were* they looking for, though?

Tightness set into her shoulders and she obsessed over someone finding the half-moon compartment in Oupie's desk. If they did, they'd assume they were hiding something, for sure. What then? A see-saw kind of conflict swayed in her gut. She *was* hiding something, though. Was it fair to expect the police to lay their cards on the table while she'd pulled hers close to her chest?

Gia clenched and unclenched her fist.

Her thoughts kept darting back to the riddle. Specifically: *Those who know thereof do not speak. Those who speak cannot know.* Not, shouldn't know, don't know or mustn't know. It said *cannot know.* Like it was a life or death thing. No matter how ridiculous that sounded. Then it occurred to her — what if it was a life or death thing? What if Oupie was hiding because he suspected someone was after him?

The more she grappled with it, the more worry wobbled through her. When Oupie sent her the key, he knew she'd search for what it opened. What if the reason he made her look was because he wanted to get the scroll out of the house? He'd known before anyone else, after all, that it wasn't him they'd buried. Which surely meant that he'd expect the police to come sniffing the moment they got a whiff of their error.

Gia clenched her fist and unclenched.

A tingle of danger shot along her neck. Could she be right? Could police be searching for the scroll? Or the key? What if they were aware of Oupie's secret passage beneath the waterfall? They'd need the key for that. Gia moved towards her bedroom door, counting to ten and trying to will her armpits to stop sweating. Fat lot of good it did. But the roly-poly policewoman turned her couch upside-down and began prowling for hideaways between the yellow giraffes sprinting across its pink fabric, and Gia reached her decision.

Say nothing.

Limping into the corridor, she made a show of leaning hard on her crutches so that no one would dream of taking them away from her and searching below the armrests. She just prayed that the childish dot of nail polish wasn't a dead giveaway. But no one noticed, and she tried to hide the smug twinge moving through her chest when she got the sense that no one suspected, either.

Gia found her dad loitering between the kitchen and living room. A pang of sympathy stiffened her chin because he looked like someone lost. When he caught sight of her watching him, he leaned against the wall with his arms knitted across his chest. Time and again, he massaged his eyelids and stared wistfully at a photograph of her mom sitting on the porch. He wasn't over it.

Gia wasn't sure he'd ever be.

It was her dad who'd taken her mom horse riding that day. He was with her when she fell. An accident that killed her and left him forever a changed man. By the time the ambulance had left the yard, its sirens dull, she already knew that she'd lost a part of him too.

'Gabriel Lance?' an officer enquired at mid-morning.

'What's this about?' Her dad's jaw set as they took him away for questioning.

Gia shoved trembling hands into her pockets when she realised how selfish she'd been these past weeks. When she lost her mom, her dad had lost his wife. When she lost Oupie, her dad had lost a friend, probably his best friend. Her thoughts ran to the memory of how many nights she'd awoken to Oupie, her dad and Elias bumping their drinks together and screaming with belly laughter. Sometimes so extreme, she'd giggled along without knowing why. Her dad hadn't laughed that way since the day Oupie had gone missing.

Not a single snort.

Gia settled into the kitchen booth, snacked on a boiled egg, changed the mulberry leaves in her silkworm box and painted each fingernail a different colour. The things she figured the police expected innocent children to do. But she kept her eyes peeled to anyone who moved about in a uniform and tried her best to eavesdrop.

By lunchtime, her dad still hadn't returned and Gia's bum had gone numb from sitting. She swung her way through the ransacked house. Books in the TV room lay peppered across the floor. Crockery stood on top of kitchen counters and food from their pantry appeared to have skulked left and right as if attempting a getaway.

Gia stopped in front of Oupie's bedroom. Someone had flipped his Persian rug back as if searching for hidden trapdoors. The cupboards were ajar, socks draped from drawers, they'd even fondled the duvet. A silver photo album sprawled on the redwood floor in direct sunlight. Gia slanted her crutches against the wall. With a heavy heart, she hobbled to retrieve it, startling at her reflection in Oupie's mirror. Pointy elbows, hair paler than potato, knobbly hips and her grandmother's hand-me-down eyes that, at the moment, held the gaze of a reprimanded puppy. Her skin pricked. She sensed someone shift in the far corner of the room.

Were the police still here? She didn't want to find herself cornered by any of *them.*

Gia took a slow step forward, stretching her neck.

Just then her nose crimped from the scent of peppermint and she caught sight of another image in the mirror — Elias. He sat on his haunches, his ear pressed against the wall between Oupie's bed and bathroom while tap-tap-tapping the brick with his knuckle.

Gia blinked. What was Elias looking for? Something hollow, that seemed obvious. Why, though? Had Elias pulled the carpet back? Was he searching for Oupie's hideout or something of Oupie's? She limped nearer, straining for a better view. And tramped on the photo album.

Fool!

In the mirror, Elias spun.

Such a fool.

Heart pounding, she looked at the ground and bent to retrieve the album.

'Gia?'

'Elias?' His sparkly shoes stopped before her so she stood up and searched for signs of guilt that she couldn't find, then waited for an explanation that never came.

'Is everything okay?' Elias whispered finally in his typical monotonous tone.

What an odd question, Gia thought. Did he mean aside from the fact that police were raiding their home? That Oupie had gone missing? Or was dead, according to some? What about her fractured foot? Did his question include that? She opted for a change of topic. 'Did police question you, Elias?'

'Yes.'

'Will they question me?'

'Probably.'

Gia gulped and inspected the ironing stripes on her godfather's shirt.

He knelt and gave her an unexpected hug, then looked at her with kind eyes. 'Sometimes, in situations such as these, I find it prudent to…' Elias paused.

Gia narrowed her eyes. 'Lie?'

Elias frowned. 'Answer the question asked. Nothing more.'

'Oh.' Her cheeks burned. 'You mean, don't offer information?'

Elias nodded. 'Get it?'

'Got it.' Gia watched him amble away, trying to fathom what information it was that he thought she had. He knew something, that was obvious. But what? She sighed, placing Oupie's album on his bedside cabinet, running her hand over it. The album had formed part and parcel of Oupie's daily routine. Every morning, he'd turn a page and celebrate Oumie's life. Gia opened it, staring at the newspaper photograph of the petite, blond girl she'd seen so many times.

The paper had published the article about Oumie in June 1962 in one of the local farming districts. The ink had greyed. She struggled to read it, but knew the story well enough to gather the gist of it. A couple of early morning walkers had found Oumie wandering along the False Bay shore, not far from Polymead Grove, in fact. Police had requested anyone with information to come forward. Oumie had worn a diamond bracelet which anyone claiming her would have had to describe. Her age was estimated at around three-years-old, too young to string sentences together, but police believed they'd established her name through some of her jabberings — Grace — and that she'd fallen down a mountain. Aside from that, she didn't remember much. Doctors concluded that she had suffered severe head trauma and memory loss. No one claimed her and in the end, police deemed that Oumie wasn't lost but abused and abandoned. She'd become a ward of the state until a preacher adopted her. Sadly, her memory had never returned. Gia stroked the image of the girl's face, glad things had tilted in her favour in the end.

Shadows had fallen across parts of the yard by the time Gia noticed police officers withdrawing from the house. She hopped her way past the kitchen, through their French doors decorated with red and green stained-glass roses, and towards where Vuyo sat on the roofed terrace with his cap on backwards. He hunched over every school book he owned, intent on doing homework with all twenty-four of his pencils. He must have forgotten they were slap-bang in the middle of the school holidays. Talk about suspicious, Gia thought.

Without looking up, Vuyo put a fist in front of his mouth, cleared his throat, then opened his hand and closed it, opened it, closed it. He jabbed a finger toward Oupie's study.

Their signal for angry grownups.

Whoever was in the there — was arguing.

Tyres crunched gravel, and Gia shuffled towards the window watching a police car roll into the driveway at the speed of a hearse. Its front passenger door opened and a sharp pang of dread squeezed Gia's chest when her godmother, Tammy Goodman, rose from the vehicle with a face so pale, she looked ill. Her long, flowing dress, the colour of the best sky, snapped in the breeze.

Friendly as a cactus, Tammy turned her back on the extended hand of the policewoman who'd stepped towards her. She opened the vehicle's rear door herself, taking a white cane from the passenger's hand.

Gia's jaw fell.

'What on earth? Why would the police want to question Bongi?' Vuyo hissed, rushing down the steps to help his grandmother.

Peculiar bone-beads adorned the stem of Bongi's neck like halters. A braided, orange dress draped to within an inch of her jewelled sandals and the matching turban she wore wrapped around her hair was traditional in these parts, and yet it created a stuffiness that suited her.

Bongi stood with her back towards them but cocked her ear as they approached, which made her gaunt, bony jaw jut to the side. She turned, tap-tap-tapping the ground with her cane as if it were a tentacle. She beckoned for Gia to approach, lifting an arm draped from wrist to elbow in bracelets made from the same eerie bone-beads.

'Come, Gia Chile. Bongi deserves a decent greeting, yes?' Bongi's velvety voice drawled, but her gaze stayed unfocused, milky, same as always. How she guessed who surrounded her remained one of life's mysteries.

Gia rushed to hug her. Bongi's beads rustled happily while she returned the embrace, smiling mischievously. Laugh lines spread along the sides of her face like the spidery grain on weathered wood. 'You missed Bongi, yes?'

'Of course.' Gia cooed. 'How did you know it was me?'

'Bongi sees many things, Chile.' Bongi continued addressing her in the term of endearment that she reserved for family.

'No, you don't,' Vuyo gurgled, embracing his grandmother tenderly.

A harmonious cackle escaped Bongi's red pair of lips. Her dark, puffy cheeks bunched, making her eyes wrinkle.

'What are you doing here?' Vuyo checked.

'Police asked Bongi to come.'

'Why? Do you know something?'

'Bongi knows many things, yes.' Bongi nodded, satisfied.

Tammy chuckled, lifting her arms. She pulled Gia to her bust with warm hands before returning her to arm's length. Her little ritual that Gia secretly loved. Tammy's bright-blue penetrating gaze slid over Gia's pink running shoe, neon-orange shorts and burgundy tie-dye shirt that she'd fastened into a knot along the hem and draped over the knob of her hip. 'You're Oumie's child, all right. Your eyes are an exact match and just like Samuel says, too big for your face,' Tammy breathed and her long twisted strands of auburn hair bobbed. She took Bongi's hand, leading her away.

Vuyo nudged Gia with his elbow and tattle-tailed. 'Detective Steele isn't mucking around. He questioned my dad for four hours. Squeezed him like a lemon! Now he's throwing both of our families together.'

'Why?'

'I dunno.'

'Did he question you?'

'Mmm, but don't worry, I'm a tough nut to crack,' Vuyo said, chest puffed out.

'They never spoke to me.'

Vuyo dashed a devious dragon glance left and right. 'Because your dad refused to give them permission, that's why. He said you've been through enough. First your mom, now Oupie, so unless Detective Steele gets a psychologist out here to sit in and supervise, the answer is no. Their shouting match carried on for ages.'

Gia turned to scowl at him. Not that she struggled to believe him. What she grappled with was her dad thinking she wasn't coping. Where would he get that idea? She hadn't breathed a word about seeing Oupie on the bridge. Not since he'd helped the doctor force a mask onto her face, and she'd almost died from giggling.

That's when it occurred to her.

What if her father didn't want police knowing that she'd insisted Oupie was alive all along? Or what if it wasn't that he didn't believe *her*, but that he didn't want anyone else knowing what she'd seen? Was it possible that she wasn't the only one keeping secrets?

Chapter 7:

Dragon head

'It's an awful idea.' Vuyo's expression flooded with disbelief.

'Awful.' Gia nodded.

'One of your worst. If we're caught-'

'Your mom will kill us.' Gia made a slicing action at the base of her neck. An image of Tammy's crossness sent a shiver down her spine.

'My mom? A real-life detective is in there! Perhaps we should mind our own beeswax.' Vuyo peered around as if worrying the walls had ears.

'Pleeeeaaaase,' Gia grovelled. 'I have need-to-knows and someone in there knows.'

'I dunno, Gia.'

'I'll do something for you.'

'Really? What?' Vuyo stepped forward, interested at once.

'Anything.'

'Anything?' he droned in a low tone that sounded danger bells.

'Well... not absolutely anything,' Gia backtracked.

'I want to camp for my birthday.'

'Outside?' Her neck and shoulders drooped. Give a boy a hand and he rips it off, Gia pouted.

Vuyo twisted his mouth to the side, lifted his wristwatch and checked the dials. 'Our deal expires in five seconds.'

'But-'

'Four... three...'

'Vuyo!'

'Two-'

'Okay! But the dogs get to sleep in my tent.' Gia poked him in the chest and seconds later, clung to his back as if she were a duffel bag.

Vuyo pitter-pattered across the wooden deck in the backyard. Hopped off, sprinted to the corner and checked the coast was crystal clear before trudging across the lawn. He weaved a path through a sea of sweet-scented rose bushes, one hunch-shouldered step at a time. 'Ouch!' Vuyo staggered and dropped her to play doctor after a vindictive thorn ripped a stripe of oozing blood-speckles into his calf.

'Shh!' Gia's guilty heart bounced. She crawled through a mucky-puddle, crouching beneath the safety of the study's window ledge.

Vuyo sidled in beside her. They waited, all stiff and awkward, senses on high alert. Gia wiped the grit from her palms onto her bum, eyeing the yard. In this place, even an animal's reaction could blow their cover. Especially the geese! She leaned her back against the wall, tilted her head and listened to muffled voices entering the room.

A scuff of a boot, the squeak of a couch. Someone coughed.

Slowly Gia came to her feet. Edging her neck out, she peered over the window ledge where a line of black ants marched around a lifeless bumble-bee.

Vuyo mirrored her action. They scrunched their eyes, squinting into the study.

The cheek of it! Detective Steele had hijacked Oupie's desk. His unruly eyebrows scouted around as if trying to flee his face while he massaged his temples and frowned over some of Oupie's papers.

Bongi had settled onto the couch. Tammy sat beside her, clutching a pot-belly cushion to her chest. She watched Detective Steele the way a hawk watches for prey.

Gia's dad loitered in the corner, engrossed with picking invisible specks of dust from his shoulder while his shaggy head of hair dangled forward on his chest. Gia wondered if he realised that his fidgeting fingers contradicted his calm-as-a-mountain-lake composure.

Elias parked in front of the door, erect as a soldier. He faced the desk at a slight angle to the window so they'd have to be careful they weren't seen, Gia concluded, because his instincts were sharper than blades.

Detective Steele pulled a document from his file with hairy fingers, looked up. 'State your name for the record, please.'

'Tammy Goodman.'

'And yours, madam?'

'Bongi Goodman.'

'How are you acquainted with Samuel George Morgan?'

'Bongi has worked at Polymead Grove ever since the factory started,' Bongi declared proudly.

Detective Steele wasted no time with idle chit-chat. He stood, strolled towards Oupie's weapons and ambled back carrying identical, banana-shaped firearms with gleaming copper barrels and redwood handles.

Vuyo flung Gia his question mark frown.

She poked out her bottom lip, rolling her shoulders. The guns seemed so random.

Detective Steele perched on the edge of Oupie's desk, legs crossed. His eyebrows did their hang-over-the-ledge thing while he looked down and stroked yellowing fingertips along the barrel of a gun. 'Do you know what this is?'

'A blunderbuss,' Tammy replied, flattening her dress.

'They've never fired a bullet, or been loaded for that matter. Why's that, do you think?'

'What's this about?'

'I can't see them properly!' Gia stretched onto her tippy-toes.

'Shh!' Vuyo tossed her a frown of daggers.

Elias stepped forward, cocking his head in Bongi's direction. 'May I?'

'Yes, of course. My apologies.' Detective Steele nodded and his face turned strawberry.

Elias placed the guns on Bongi's lap and Vuyo dropped his jaw, exaggerating the action, eyes glinting like a mischievous elf as Bongi inspected the guns with fingers that seemed to carry more skin than they carried bone.

'They have emblems on their sides. Three each,' Detective Steele drawled.

'Bongi feels them, yes.'

'Those emblems are how Samuel George Morgan knew for a fact that the blunderbuss Tammy Goodman presented to an artefact dealer for valuation wasn't the same one they returned to her.'

'What? No. No. I checked it.' Tammy launched a defensive, squeezing the pot-belly cushion until it appeared close to bursting.

Shock waves rumbled down Gia's spine. Had it been a poor choice of words, or had Detective Steele meant to imply that he'd spoken to Oupie? When was that exactly? Is that why he was focused on Oupie's guns instead of his disappearance? Is it possible that he knew where Oupie was?

'Why did you remove Samuel's weapon from its case?' Detective Steele tossed Tammy an accusatory stare.

'I wanted to surprise him with its value for his birthday. Samuel said it was worthless, but…' Tammy shrugged. 'They don't look worthless.'

'So… you never had permission?' An imperious eyebrow leapt to attention.

'I never stole it, Detective,' Tammy snapped. 'We're family!'

'Are you?'

'We're as good as.'

'What did the dealer say? Were you right, Mrs Goodman? *Are* Samuel's guns valuable?'

'Get to your point.' Tammy's gaze flashed with intelligence.

'Samuel confronted them. A company called Worldwide Valuations Incorporated. Three brothers who travel about doing assessment road-shows inviting the public to bring them antiques, heirlooms or any relic that might be valuable. They denied his allegation, so he came to me demanding I retrieve his weapon immediately. He said the gun was cast in the early nineteen hundreds and only twelve exist. And he suggested that if those dealers switched his artefact, they'd probably substituted other people's property too. I talked to them. They not only denied Samuel's allegation, but Deon Sanderson, the youngest of the brothers, implied that Samuel had stolen the blunderbuss to begin with.'

'Oh, please,' Tammy twanged.

'As if!' Gia hissed and Bongi tilted her head.

The action never went unnoticed.

Elias turned to examine the window and Vuyo slapped a hand over Gia's mouth, jerking her downwards. They flopped between roses, gasping. And because she couldn't help her stupid self, Gia batted his hand away. 'We need to get a look at those embl-'

'Shut up!' Vuyo groused.

The window shot open.

Gia's belly muscles clenched. She got a whiff of peppermint mingled with the remnants of Oupie's tobacco odour and covered her nose and mouth with her palms, trying not to make breathing sounds. Elias' hand hovered on the latch. They were sitting ducks. All he needed to do was lean forward, and they'd be found out. Would he call them out in front of Detective Steele?

They waited.

'Something the matter?' Detective Steele drawled.

'Just needed some air.' Elias pulled his hand back.

'What did you do after that?' Tammy's voice asked. 'I hope you never fell for that tall story.'

Gia risked going onto her haunches. She slithered with her chest against the wall and squinted back over the window ledge, careful not to squash the little task force of ants who were now shifting the bumble-bee to her right. Elias had moved — small mercy. He leaned against the windowsill with his back towards them. Gia used him to shield her prying actions. She moved bit by bit sideways for a view of the room.

Tammy had scrunched her eyes into slits, studying Detective Steele solemnly.

'I didn't have time to do anything, Mrs Goodman. The day after that Samuel George Morgan rolled his car.'

'But?' Gia's dad prompted with a bitter smile.

'But a week after that, Worldwide Valuations Incorporated filed a missing person report for their youngest brother, Deon Sanderson.'

A jolt of comprehension sliced Gia to the bone.

There was only one reason Deon Sanderson's disappearance would apply to the conversation. It didn't take a fairy to figure out what. She locked eyes with Vuyo and they turned frozen with listening. The silence in the study seemed to prickle through the window and Gia had just begun resenting Detective Steele's dramatic manner when she clicked she was getting exactly what she needed — information.

Detective Steele cocked his head to the side. 'Would any of you like to guess the date on which Deon Sanderson went missing?'

Vuyo took Gia's hand.

'Sweet Mother of...' Tammy's bright-blue eyes had gone teary. She collapsed onto her cushion, making the sound of a puncturing balloon. Bongi reached out, patting her back.

Vuyo kept Gia's hand. They didn't need to be city kids to understand this conversation had just leapt sideways. It was oh-so-obvious which day Detective Steele was referring to — the day Oupie had rolled his car.

'*Was* it Deon Sanderson that you found in Samuel's vehicle?' Gia's dad checked and Vuyo leaned in. He was all ears, everybody was.

'Indeed.' Detective Steele pulled a photograph from his files and pointed at what looked like black smudges on a piece of charred metal. 'And the burn patterns show the use of an accelerant.'

With earth-shattering clarity, Gia suddenly understood what the interview was about. Detective Steele wasn't hunting a missing person or solving the identity of a charred corpse, neither was he searching for a key nor keeping an eye out for a scroll. He was after a cold-blooded killer and he'd set his sights on Oupie. She didn't believe it. Not for a minute. Just because detectives went around mumbling things didn't make them true. But it was alarming to think that someone else believed it.

'I resent your insinuation,' Gia's dad whispered coolly. 'What was Deon Sanderson doing on our bridge in the first place?'

'Exactly!' Tammy jeered. 'It's inconceivable for him to have randomly been there.'

Gia could have jumped up and kissed them right there. Why hadn't she thought of that?

'If Deon Sanderson's disappearance involved Samuel, I can guarantee you that he wouldn't risk rolling a vehicle with his granddaughter in it. No bloody way.' Gia's father twisted his mouth to the side, shook his head.

'Mmm. Well, nothing strange there.' Detective Steele cracked his knuckles, giving Gia the impression that he hadn't been expecting their agreement. 'What strikes me as strange, though, is that Samuel has licences and ownership documents for every weapon in that case except these two firearms. A remarkable coincidence, wouldn't you agree?'

Nobody said anything. Nobody dared.

But Gia spotted that her dad didn't shy away from Detective Steele's gaze the way Tammy did, and she couldn't help wonder if she'd misjudged his silent manner. Perhaps it was a strength and not weakness? Sometimes Tammy caught them jabbering during lessons, and she'd lecture them about fools that spoke while wise men listened. Maybe her dad's manner implied he was a listener.

'The thing is, Gabriel. If I can't confirm that these guns belong to Samuel, I can't disregard Deon Sanderson's accusation. Not after what's happened. You understand that, surely? And the way things stand, if these guns *are* as rare and as old as Samuel implied they were, they serve as a motive for murder.'

'Well, my logic says that if Samuel planned to kill anyone, he wouldn't have spoken to you first,' Gia's father replied, calm, collected. Direct.

Gia put a hand over her mouth, covering her smile.

'Irrespective. There's obviously something about one of these guns that triggered Samuel's suspicion. Which is why I'm taking them with me.' Detective Steele slid a document across the desk towards Gia's father. Then came to his feet.

'You can't do that!' Tammy objected.

'As a matter of fact, Mrs Goodman, I can. Sign there, please.' Detective Steel tapped the book he'd presented. 'I've attached photographs of each item, for your reference. It's worth mentioning, though, Gabriel — if you can't produce the ownership records for these weapons by the time Forensics have completed their analysis, I won't be able to return them to you. Unlicenced firearms are illegal, after all.'

Gia's dad signed his squiggle, but his jaw set. 'Shouldn't you be arranging a search party for Samuel?'

'If that's where the evidence leads, sure.' Detective Steele peeled off the top copy of his document and placed it next to the photographs of Oupie's firearms that he'd left on the desk. And tucking his bounty under his armpit, 'I'll see myself out, shall I? Good day, Mrs Goodman.'

Gia itched to get her hands on the photographs. The grownups' spitefully stayed put.

A door opened.

Closed.

A car door banged.

An engine started.

And Elias murmured, 'Mom?'

Bongi bobbed, a slur of a smile playing on her lips. 'The emblems on those guns don't match.'

'I knew it.' Vuyo tossed her a satisfied smirk.

Confusion squirted through Gia, and her sixth sense questioned why the grownups in her life seemed to act so secretively. Elias especially.

Gia's dad put his hands on his hips. Clenching his jaw, he grunted, 'Why didn't you say anything when Detective Steele was here? You make it sound as if we have something to hide.'

'When the fox hears the rabbit scream, it comes running. But it isn't to help, Chile,' Bongi drawled seductively.

'You heard the man, Gabriel. Detective Steele already believes Samuel's guilty. He didn't come to help,' Elias motivated.

'Well, if that's true… I'm going to visit Samuel's attorney at first light. See what our options are.'

'Yes. Good.' Bongi nodded. 'The dragonhead wasn't even an excellent copy, I'm surprised you never noticed, Tammy Chile.'

'Dragon head?' Gia mouthed, puckering a quizzical brow. She stood on her tippy-toes, squinting at the photographs on Oupie's desk.

Guns that had always been in Oupie's case dollying up the room came into focus. Gia examined the moulded dragon heads. Their tails snuggled round the gun's handles and her blood ran cold. It was a fight not crying out. She yanked Vuyo by his arm and dropped to the ground. 'That dragon head matches the dragon on the gate beneath the bent wall! That's why it was familiar.'

'Are you sure?' Vuyo sucked in a breath.

'Positive. It's identical!'

Chapter 8:

Where fate began its trend

Dawn hadn't quite arrived. A tang of damp, manured earth taunted her nostrils. The creak of crickets and the odd rustling of shrubs kept Gia's eyes alert and ever-scouting through a fog so thick it had practically turned gooey. She hated the way it floated off the sea entangling the farm in a noiseless ghost-grey and maybe-deadly vapour.

Vuyo skulked about in a lime-green shirt and orange peak-cap that said, *It wasn't me*. As if anyone would believe it. He shone his torch into his mouth, flicking the switch with multiple clickity-clacks. 'Whhooo,' he teased and his cheeks turned tangerine, making Gia's toes curl.

Boys!

'How did you smuggle yourself out so early?' Vuyo checked. 'I can't remember *you* ever waking *me* up.'

'I didn't. My dad left for Cape Town at six so, mwah.' Gia gestured down the length of her body. 'Had time for a chinwag with Google *and…*' She flicked her eyebrows, plucking a wad of papers from the pocket of her lilac dungarees as if she'd pulled them from a hat. 'Ta-da!' Gia sang in the cheeriest voice she was able to conjure.

'Detective Steel's photographs.' Vuyo seized them. Shone his torch at the page. 'You stole them?' His eyes became engorged, but they danced with praise.

'I made copies. Duh!'

'The guns look the same to me.' Vuyo's forehead crumpled.

'Me too. We know they aren't though, because Bongi wouldn't make a mistake like that. But get this. Emblems were used to personalise weapons, and Google says that each of them stands for something specific.'

'Such as?'

'The top emblem on a shotgun was the owner's family crest, the gunmaker logo is in the middle and the bottom mark represented the country of origin. But! And it's a big but. In the olden days, royals, nobles or people with so much money that they didn't know what to do with it, replaced the country of origin with the number of the vessel they intended storing the guns on. If the owner of a shotgun used all three emblems-'

'It was super unique!'

'Exactly. Now check the photos again.'

Vuyo exaggerated a dropped jaw, his eyes glittering. 'This third emblem is a number, V-double-zero-seven.'

'Bingo!'

The fog had wisped and thinned by the time they arrived at the pool below the thunderous waterfall. In its place, dark-grey storm clouds gathered in swarms, allowing an occasional wink of sunlight through. They hid the go-ped, her helmet and the bicycle between bushes, and with Vuyo's help, Gia crossed the rocks. She made her way across the ledge and towards the cave entrance. But he egged her on, acting as if they were on a scavenger hunt. He even ordered the dogs to hustle. Being locked up seemed to have left the poor things scarred. They'd peed on pebbles, dug in the dirt, rearranged some shrubs. As if appreciating the outdoors that bit more. It took a considerable amount of begging to coax them through the waterfall.

The cave enveloped them with the dank darkness that Gia remembered. She scrunched her nose and rubbed her goose bumped arms while Vuyo danced and bobbed the torchlight back and forth before prancing up the red-brick steps two at a time. When Gia caught up, he was engrossed with a forensic inspection of the dragon head, comparing it side by side to the photocopy she'd given him. The likeness was unmistakable.

'Told you,' she crooned.

'What do you think it means?'

'Dunno, but it's no coincidence that it matches the handle on Oupie's guns.'

Their conversation plunged into silence and Vuyo fished the key from his pocket, licking his lips as he slid it into the gate's lock.

It jammed.

He wiggled it back and forth until it screeched open with a kind of *nei-ei-eigh*!

Gia bounced on her good foot, did a little dance, and Vuyo leaned his ear through the arch.

He waited, then pulled the riddle from the rucksack's side pocket. '*When your shadow grows tall.* Done. *Enter beneath the bent wall.* Did that too. *Follow the path to the end.*' He pointed at the spiralling staircase. '*Find the place where fate began its trend.* We're almost there, Gia. I'll go first, though. Just in case.'

They tiptoed one deliberate footstep at a time, climbing a storey of winding steps, Gia estimated. Two at the most. Her breathing increased, her heart slammed, and she strained her ears, scouting for movement that she was both eager for and terrified of. Vuyo's eyes hunted the vicinity, suspicious.

They came out of the cave behind the crest of the waterfall. It was as she'd expected. They were now on top of the mountain bordering the ocean. The swooning scent of briny sea licked their faces, trickling water branched and slunk through giant reeds that stood tall and proud, thick as braided fabric. From somewhere inside them, a rustling choir of insects tested the limits of their lungs. A chameleon watched, waited.

Gia buzzed with excitement from the anticipation of seeing Oupie again. She scamper-hobbled to the end of the pathway for a peek around the reeds. She'd been saving the biggest hug ever. She stopped and fought the trickle of uncertainty that began spiralling through her. It was an extraordinary thing, doubting her eyeballs. Gia blinked and blinked, wrinkling her nose at the sight of a meadow the size of a hockey field.

Boulders ran along the edge of the cliff, shielding a flat part of ground from both the sea and the farm as if fortifying it. Seagulls shrieked and wailed at their intrusion, butterflies took to the air, knee-high grass whispered warnings and a flock of guinea fowl scattered like cockroaches the moment Jinja rushed to introduce herself.

'A plateau?' Vuyo frowned.

Gia gaped at the sight. The sea was so close she tasted it on her lips, but she glimpsed only bits of it over the boulders. It wasn't hard to imagine that the ships with their bare masts nodding on the horizon wouldn't be able to see her either.

Vuyo jogged towards the boulders. He hoisted himself onto a low bulge and offered Gia an arm when she caught up.

'Is it high?'

'Very.'

'Oh.'

'But the rocks are too close together for us to fall through. I'll hold you. Promise.'

Careful to avoid seagull droppings while shifting aside a creeper that explored the cracks between rocks, Gia gripped Vuyo's palm that was firm and steadying. She pulled herself up and slithered on her bum across the warm rock-face.

'Easy does it.' Vuyo looped an arm over her shoulder and they snuggled likes peas peering over a perilous long-drop which overlooked False Bay, a golden-arched beach and a cliff-side pounded by angry waves roughly three storeys below them. 'I'm not sure I get it,' Vuyo hummed, his face stacked with doubt as he lowered Gia back onto the ground a short while later. 'What is this place? It's man made, that's for sure. Because its far to exact a square to be natural. Why shield an empty field from the bay, though? And from the farm? From anything?'

Gia recycled the thought, churning it over and over. There was little doubt Vuyo was right. Everything around them seemed… wrong. Why did the plateau exist? Why all the effort to hide it? All she understood for sure was that something bigger than she'd expected was going on. Like choosing a puzzle with three-hundred pieces only to discover that someone had thrown a thousand jigsaw bits into the box. What's obvious was that Oupie had been keeping secrets. From them, from her, Gia the fool. And they had to be terrible if he'd lock them away. For the first time, the little demon in her questioned if a secret was the same as a lie, because why did people always seem to lie when they kept secrets? She fought to send the lurching feeling back where it came from.

'There!' Vuyo pointed and Gia swivelled.

Built below a ledge of a boulder, probably for wind protection, nestled a wooden, sunburned hut. It didn't have a door. Birds had thinned away its thatched terrace over time and it peeled paint like a sunbather peeled skin. In the veld next to it, Protea bushes were in full bloom, their flowers the colour of a dog's tongue.

'That must be *the place where fate began its trend*,' Vuyo hollered and joined the dogs as they charged.

It was empty.

Mostly.

Cobweb mansions were woven into the corners. A pile of rope lay twirled on the floor beside a rickety rocking bench and a piece of shredded canvas tarp that had a pockmarked edge as if it had survived long wet spells. They were all covered with a mulch of disintegrating leaves.

Gia watched the hurricane of activity. Jinja sniffed and sneezed. Nina lapped water from a puddle before hijacking a corner of the porch and settling into a twitchy snooze. It had to be exhausting being so awesome, Gia decided. Vuyo stamped the floor and banged the walls, as boys do. The hut creaked and groaned, clearly terrified. 'Another clue must be hidden somewhere. I just can't believe the riddle's a dead-end.' He shone his torchlight between panels.

'You won't find anything.' Gia turned away, sighing.

'How do you know?' Vuyo smarted.

'Because fate is something that happens on its own. You don't build a hut and then call it fate.'

Vuyo cupped a hand over his mouth and hollered, 'HELLO!'

'Shh! Are you mad?'

An echo came back. *Hello, hello, hello, shh, shh, shh, mad, mad, mad.*

Vuyo shrugged and waved his arm in a half-circle. 'Oupie wouldn't have missed that. Actually, I think that he would have heard the gate opening. He isn't here, Gia.'

'He must be! He wouldn't just leave me, Vuyo.'

'There's nothing here.'

'Then why guard it?' She flicked her palms to the heavens.

'Maybe you're wrong about-'

'I can't be because — hello — he sent the key, and this is where it led.' She twirled in a circle, gesturing and swallowing hard.

Vuyo sighed. 'Look around you, though. Does this make sense? Any of it? At all?'

Gia was unprepared for this. Solve the riddle, find Oupie, give him the scroll. That was the extent of her grand plan. So, what now? If Oupie wasn't here, where could he be? Somewhere deep inside her, a haunting idea kindled to life and despite her head not fancying it, the skin across her shoulders tightened and she struggled to stop it from igniting. It had to be how Jack felt about his beanstalk. She knew at once that her idea was worth exploring. 'Vuyo, what if Oupie's riddle isn't about finding something? What if it's about seeing something?'

Vuyo's forehead bunched. Black eyes that understood her all too well, examined her before his face cracked into a greedy-goblin grin. 'Are you suggesting what I think you're suggesting?'

'If we were supposed to find something, it would be here. And if the riddle was about finding Oupie, *he'd* be here.'

'That scroll could be dangerous, Gia. We barely dodged that knife last time. Who knows where we'll end up? It might be somewhere worse than a dungeon. You know that, right?'

'I know. But the scroll and the key are the only things Oupie gave us. He wouldn't have done that and then sent us on this merry mission without a reason.' Gia spied around the plateau one more time. Took the leap of faith. 'It doesn't matter what Oupie's involved in, Vuyo. Or even if he's guilty. We can ask him about that type of thing later. We must assume that he's in some kind of trouble and that he sent us the key because he thinks we can help. He's family! That's all that matters, isn't it?'

Vuyo didn't reply.

Gia removed the scroll from her crutch. He made no attempt to stop her while she slid it from its tube. She stretched out her arm. 'Ready?'

He swallowed, dropped his backpack onto the ground and took Gia's hand, gripping her fingers between his. 'As I'll ever be,' he whispered, trembling with anticipation.

She let her crutches fall. Using her index finger and thumb, Gia unrolled the chalky parchment.

Wind gusted.

An icy chill lashed their faces. Gia's senses swamped with the sound of a roaring sea. Waves crashed over her head. She lost her footing. And went barrelling across a wooden deck of a ship as it smashed into the foot of a mountain.

Chapter 9:

The missing cap

The vessel jerked. It slanted towards the port side.

Gia opened her mouth to scream.

Splash!

Her neck snapped back and her belly stung from the shock of hard, frosty water that she broke through square-on. Like a human piece of driftwood, waves snatched her left, up, right, down. She kicked and kicked, ignoring the pain stabbing her foot. The airy foam of her moonboot swelled into a lead balloon and pulled her down like an anchor.

You can do it. You can do it! The thought ricocheted through her head as rocks tumbled down the sides of her face. A chain grated across the ship's keel. Gia kicked harder and harder. Her moonboot grew heavier. Sunlight twinkled from the world above the water's surface as if she was drowning in a snow globe and with crystal clarity. It was then she realised she couldn't do it. Her battle was lost. Her thrashing halted. Her heart kept hammering, but her body dropped.

The twinkle faded. Things turned dark and icy. Gia slipped into something that was neither awake nor asleep. For a second, she even imagined hearing her mom calling. The water rocked and a wink of light reappeared. Tiny black polka dots emerged. They multiplied as she tried blinking her salt singed eyes. Behind them, Vuyo materialised, moving his arms with a frog-like motion. He pointed at something. But honestly, she didn't have the strength. Gia closed her eyes for a much-needed second.

Vuyo punched her.

A well-timed karate chop where her wrist joined her palm. Gia's clenched fist startled open and released her grip of the scroll.

As if by abracadabra the sea vanished, glorious sunlight brushed her cheeks and her startled wits recognised that they'd returned to the plateau. She swayed a little and fell to her knees as her stomach clenched. Hunching into a ball, she retched until her ribs ached and she'd written a mental note to never again take warm, sweet air for granted.

'Breathe!' Vuyo knelt beside her. His hair stuck to his face but panic, bewilderment and gobsmacked disbelief are what Gia saw scribbled across it. 'Just breathe!' He patted her on the back, his teeth chattering as if they too had something to say.

'We were on that — *hic* — ship,' she croaked.

'I know. Look at the ground, it's soaked, but only this small patch. How weird is that?' Vuyo stooped to pick up her crutches.

'So then, we didn't go into the scroll, the vision — *hic* — came out of it?'

'I dunno. I don't understand why such a little water came out.' He helped her up.

Gia tucked her crutches under her armpits, hissing a sharp 'Ssssss' as she applied pressure onto her moonboot. She bit her lip and tried to keep it from wobbling.

'Are you okay?' Vuyo stepped closer and when Gia nodded, he twisted in a circle. 'Where's my cap?'

Their eyeballs orbited the plateau like vultures.

'It couldn't be stuck in-' A chill shivered through Gia's chest, she noticed goosebumps sprouting on Vuyo's neck.

There was a lengthy pause.

Vuyo's eyes stalked the area for a second time. 'My cap's gone, Gia. If it's stuck in that vision, what's to say that we can't get stuck in there too? Why would Oupie risk putting us in that much danger?' Vuyo shouted, his voice shrill with panic.

'It's a magic scroll, Vuyo. He probably didn't know everything about it,' Gia howled staunch in Oupie's defence and yet, she wasn't sure for how much longer she'd be able to keep up these pole vaults of faith. A tear slipped down her cheek and she wiped it briskly.

'I'm sorry.' Vuyo hugged her to his side and smeared a knuckle through the wetness beneath her eyelashes. 'We'll figure it out, okay. We've figured out so much already.'

Gia leaned against him, sniffling. She hoped with all her might that he wasn't just saying that. Their short run of successes had obviously petered out, but oddities were still piling up and they didn't have any more clues. What did the ship in the scroll's vision mean? Was it related to anything? How come the dragon on Oupie's blunderbuss matched the dragon on the gate? Were they also linked? And why weren't Oupie's guns licenced? What would make Deon Sanderson accuse Oupie of stealing them? How did he get into Oupie's car? And strangest of all, how come his brothers hadn't reported him missing straight away? That was weird, wasn't it? Why did they wait a week? Could they have argued about the value of the weapons? Who deserved the greater share? That made much more sense than what Detective Steele had implied, Gia decided.

'At the *very least,* Oupie must have known what the scroll would show us, Gia. It wouldn't make sense for him to give it to us otherwise,' Vuyo reasoned.

'If that's true, these visions have to be important. *Really* important for Oupie to risk our lives like that.' Gia crumpled her nose. 'And they can't be random, they've got to fit together somehow.'

'They're as random as dragons to me. It's not as if there's a playlist for us to pick what we want to see.'

Gia tested her foot, gnawing over Vuyo's comment. It was sore but grin and bearable so she shuffled towards the scroll that weirdly, didn't have a drop of water on it. 'Do you think that crash happened?'

'So what if it did? What difference does it make?' Vuyo untied his silky hair. He squeezed a river of briny water out of it and with the shake of his head tossed it over his shoulders.

Gia watched it fall into a rippling curtain that stretched half-way to his waist. 'No difference. I was just wondering how it picks what to show us.' She hunched over the scroll, cautious now. 'One minute we were chatting about ships and how their numbers were sometimes stamped onto guns and the next thing…' Her words trailed off. 'Almost as if the scroll was-' She looked up with a sharp gasp.

Listening? Vuyo mouthed, tapping his ear.

So what if she was being stupid? How was she supposed to know what magic could or couldn't do? The scroll had to have a method and eavesdropping seemed as good as any. Gia tried to recall mentioning the word dungeon before opening it in the study - couldn't. Oupie didn't have it in him to kill a man, that she knew, but he *was* involved in something and she was determined as iron to figure out what. Right *now*, it meant listening to her sixth sense, which hinted the scroll could help. She slid it back into its tube and wedged it into her crutch. 'Let's chat with Bongi because if we can figure out how the scroll's magic works, we can use its visions to our advantage.'

Vuyo smiled a cat smile. 'We might as well. There's a storm coming, anyway.' He pointed at the grey, woollen sky that appeared to be breeding rain clouds. 'And I'm starving.'

Gia staggered back across the rocks, her moonboot singing squelch-squelch with every step. Helped by Vuyo's supporting hands, she wobbled her way up the riverbank. Every step became a mind-over-matter battle because her injured foot flat-out refused to bear any weight.

They'd begun pushing the bike and go-ped towards the road when Nina whipped up her head and growled. A deep growl. As if angry on purpose.

Ahead of them, a tall, grizzly faced fellow with a flushed face and greying corkscrew hair ambled along dressed in khaki trousers and a used-to-be white shirt. Droplets of sweat ran along the ridge of his forehead and his clothes were sprinkled with so much dust that he appeared to have leopard-crawled from the beach. Worst of all, he was muttering so loudly to himself that he didn't seem to hear Nina.

His presence pricked that odd spot at the base of Gia's neck, the spot that made her gut triple-guess. What was he doing there? Why hadn't he stopped at the house? What if he was one of the Sanderson brothers? He wasn't lost. No way! It was impossible to lose your bearings on a farm that had one main road, with smaller ones all branching off it and one side of the entire property bordering the sea.

Especially if you were a grownup.

Quick-thinking Vuyo tapped a finger across his lips. He propped the go-ped and bicycle against a fallen oak, grabbed Gia's crutches and slung an arm round her waist. They hopped from the road in super-secrecy mode and used the first tree-trunk as a lookout post, despite the hum of a low hanging beehive.

There was no time to be picky.

A cracking twig betrayed them.

Chapter 10:

Grizzly faced stranger

Grizzly abandoned his discussion with Mister Invisible. Gia's eyes widened when he froze. Nina must have sensed her fright because she snarled through her teeth, her nose and mouth flesh pulling into ripples.

Grizzly swung around, planting his legs apart. He glared at Nina with a mutinous expression, knees bent. In a fluid movement, he dropped his backpack, stooped, snapped gravel from the ground and flung it at Nina's snout.

Talk about poking the bear! No way would Nina stand for that, Gia realised, watching as her dog's neck hairs rose into a ridge of retaliation. Nina lowered her front legs and before Gia could blink, she charged. Jinja began barking a minor symphony of fury as if egging her mother on, and it worked because Nina launched into the air, lunging upwards. She snapped at Grizzly's nose, didn't get it, didn't care. Her teeth sank into the cactus-like beard sprouting on his chin.

'Oouuch!' Grizzly whacked Nina on the nose, staggered and thumped over onto his bum.

'We've got to help him.' Gia grabbed Vuyo's arm.

'No way! He shouldn't be here, and Nina could turn on us. It's dangerous. *She's* dangerous when she's like this.'

Gia understood the science of avoiding dog fights, but what if doing nothing made matters worse? She wracked her brain, dismayed, but Nina, who was now frothing at the mouth, charged again. Grizzly coiled his legs into his chest like they were springs and thrust, flinging her off balance. Jinja rushed to the rescue, of course, pinning Grizzly's ankle like a bug to the ground before attempting to shake it, as dogs do.

'We *have* to help him, Vuyo.'

'No!' Vuyo's jaw set.

'What if she grabs his neck? What then?'

Grizzly punched and kicked. He seized his backpack, popped a quick-release clip, and dug his hand into its belly. The brief lull in Nina's attack when Jinja went for Grizzly's other leg was all the time the devil needed to wrench free a curved object and raise it.

It's the moment Gia realised he held a gun. 'No!' she surged from behind her lookout tree.

Too late.

Grizzly brought the wooden butt down onto Nina's leg, full-force.

A sickening snap clapped and Nina's leg went limp in the middle. She howled a sound of pure terror, slumped in the front and began a three-legged limp towards the house, yelping each time she moved.

Jinja's nerve gave up the ghost. She made a run for it. And as if the sky objected, it dropped its first *BOOM-flash-flash-BOOM* of thunder and lightning.

Only when Vuyo slapped a hand over her mouth, ramming her against the tree-trunk with the force of his panic did Gia realise that she'd drawn Grizzly's attention to them. Her heart hammered. She stared an apology into Vuyo's freaked-out eyes.

Grizzly had already swung into action. He staggered to his feet. Most likely, he was used to operating in a world of chaos and mayhem. For a heart-stopping instant, Gia came face-to-face with the gleaming barrel of a gun.

The planet ground to a halt.

An eerie sullenness fell upon the afternoon. Upon her life!

Gia swallowed and clenched her fist.

Vuyo's body trembled against hers, but he stepped back and turned to face Grizzly. After what seemed like a lifetime, Grizzly scoffed and lowered the gun.

Gia's gaze followed the movement of the weapon with hawk-sharp eyes and her tummy bounced. A blunderbuss! And snap! A dragon head matching the one on Oupie's gun curled round its redwood handle. Vuyo spotted the anomaly too. He tossed her a questioning gaze, pulling his eyes wide.

Grizzly picked up on the gesture. 'What? What was that look about? This?' He lifted the blunderbuss and gave it a waggle before examining them as if they were insects in a jar. 'You've seen a gun like it before. You know Samuel Morgan, don't you?'

Gia blinked. How odd. He'd spoken with such a peculiar accent, it took a good-long while for her stunned brain to decipher the words. She wasn't sure what to make of the nugget of info he'd dropped, though. Did he know Oupie? Or only know of him? What was it about these blunderbuss guns that fascinated everyone so? And where did Grizzly get his from?

Somewhere a gull cried and scores of guinea fowls launched into screeching the warning songs of their feathered people, which was about as helpful as waving the red flag with her feet.

The left-over look of heightened exertion receded from Grizzly's face, turning his flushed skin vampire pale. Wherever he came from, it seemed apparent he didn't get much sun. And by the sweat drenching his shirt, Gia guessed he'd been trudging around for a while. Why, though? What did he want?

Grizzly stretched his neck, squinting at Gia over Vuyo's shoulder. His jaw fell. He gave a startled gasp. 'Oh my-'

'This is private property.' Vuyo cut him off.

'You have the same-'

'You're trespassing!' Vuyo hauled out his no-nonsense voice.

Grizzly glared at them as if it was a standoff. Gia interpreted the action as meaning that he didn't care whose property he'd happened upon. He moved to retrieve his backpack, wincing the moment he put pressure onto his foot. He bent suddenly, putting the gun on the ground beside him before rolling his trousers to inspect his wound. 'Has that dog had its shots?' he growled.

The man-beast was barely wounded, Gia decided. She hoped his leg was painful, at least as painful as Nina's. He deserved it for what he'd done to her. Her leg would take weeks to set, and that's if her dad got to it soon.

She clenched her fist when it occurred to her that Grizzly didn't regard them as a threat. He wouldn't have looked away if he did.

Gia squinted at the blunderbuss, recalling how her dad said a person shouldn't point a gun at someone unless they'd pull the trigger. Exactly why he never had one. Is that why Grizzly had lowered the weapon? Or was it because he didn't like pointing it at children? Irrespective, it seemed sensible to assume their safety wasn't his priority. Gia shivered with unease. It left her with no illusion about what she had to do — find a way out of this boiling cauldron.

Grizzly spat on his hand and rubbed it into his wound, engrossed.

A brainwave emerged from the room-for-doubt corner of Gia's mind. She elbowed Vuyo in the ribs. He glanced sideways, and she pointed her index finger upwards before pushing her hand forward.

With a minuscule movement of his head, Vuyo peered at the droning beehive not far above them. His Adam's apple jerked up and down and his forehead crumpled but his jaw set and he cocked his chin towards the go-ped, mouthing, *'Can. You. Get. To. It?'*

Gia got his meaning straight away. It was a risky plan, one that couldn't be trusted. If the hive fell, crazy off the grid the bees would be! And there was no guarantee they'd go for Grizzly. How many stings would it take to kill a child? Did anybody know? Gia wondered. Her leg was strong enough to walk, but run? Doubtful. And she'd only just learned to ride the go-ped. What if she took a tumble? She wished she'd put her helmet on.

She eyed Grizzly nursing his leg. What choice did she have, though? They *had* to get away from this man, and the hive gave them that chance. Gia exhaled slowly. Now wasn't the time to consider grazed elbows, bruised knees, broken necks or the off-chance of Grizzly being allergic to bees.

Grizzly's most obvious escape route would be the river, because - Gia bet - he could swim. Which left them the opposite direction. If only it wasn't uphill. But if Nina could make it… Gia clamped her teeth. Nodded.

Grizzly spat on his sleeve and dabbed his leg.

Taking a snail's pace, Gia tried shielding Vuyo's movements. She snuck him a crutch which he hoisted into the air.

A spiteful branch stuck its nose in. It hooked beneath the shoulder support.

Vuyo gave it a wriggle. It snubbed his budge and a bee buzzed over the brim, parking on his cheekbone with a villainous growl of warning.

Oh dear, thought Gia.

Vuyo ended up with his arms above his head and a face that screamed of desperation. One glance, or tiny poke, was all it would take to blow their blind twinge of hope.

Gia counted the paces when she began pondering a rugby tackle as an option. They could wrestle for the gun. It *was* two against one. What would be the point, though? It's not as if she'd use it. What kind of maniac carried a shotgun only to use its butt instead of its barrel, anyway? Gia's eyebrows shot up. Had they been out-foxed? Was it possible that Grizzly's gun wasn't loaded?

She peered at his grimy, shades-of-plum wound that oozed globules of blood. Maybe, huge maybe, if she reached the go-ped she wouldn't be the slowest hop-a-long around.

Grizzly rolled down his trousers. Looked up.

A shrill shivered across Gia's shoulders. She cupped her hands under the stump of the trapped crutch and rammed it skywards, putting all her strength and loathing into it.

The interfering branch cracked.

The crutch switched direction. Instead of hitting the beehive at the back and tipping it onto Grizzly, it punched the box side on.

An angry vibration stirred inside it.

It crashed onto the ground beside Gia.

Chapter 11:

Little assassins

The world exploded with the concentrated hum of swarming.

'Ouch!' Vuyo slapped his cheek.

A bee stung Gia's arm. A tingling, icy pain took root in her elbow.

Heart lurching, she ditched the crutch and bolted. It was obvious the little assassins weren't sending out a welcoming party. The go-ped screamed to her like the beacon of a lighthouse. Without bothering to check on Grizzly, and with the help of her left-over crutch, she stumbled as fast as her good-foot, bad-foot could carry her. Whatever happened, she *had* to be faster than him.

Buzz.

The planet was abuzz.

A bee zapped her leg, another poked its needle into her neck, its friend jabbed her butt, and yet another buzzed and buzzed before stabbing her in the hand. She stopped counting after that. Little as they were, could have been daggers. It's then she realised she was screaming, had been all along.

Gia mounted the go-ped, punched the switch. The little engine responded with the roar of a lazy lawnmower and — small mercy — it smoked! *Bees don't like smoke!* Blinking through her sob of boiling tears, she focused every inch of her willpower on keeping her hands clenched on the handlebars. Her knuckles whitened. She tried forcing herself to calm.

Vuyo tried no such thing. 'Go! Go! Go!' he yelled like no ordinary kind of fruitcake. Ditching his backpack and hurtling past her in the direction of the farmhouse, he slapped his arms and legs with a randomly made-up technique as if living his nightmare.

Gia's getaway vehicle spluttered and with her heart still drum-rolling, she pulled her chin to her chest and wrenched the accelerator back. The go-ped almost choked. It hit a speed bump, wobbling, wobbling. Gia gulped and, tightening her grip, bent her knees to keep her balance. She knew better than to slow down. A bee that couldn't land, couldn't sting. Simple mechanics. She spent the next few seconds wishing she'd worn her helmet.

Up the hill.

Still screaming.

Go-ped jerking.

The distance between them and the hive grew with the blur of each tree. From the river, someone shouted words that kids weren't supposed to hear. It seemed the mob had followed Grizzly after all. He did deserve it the most, so Gia decided anyway.

She caught sight of Nina. 'Run! Nina, Run!' And a minute later, the roof of their barn.

Eighty metres and closing.

Her chest burned.

Sixty metres.

Past the apple orchard.

After what could have been three lifetimes, the buzzing dwindled. As did her frenzy. Unexpectedly, Gia's senses were alerted to the drip and plop of sporadic rain.

Yay! Bees don't play in the rain!

Forty metres.

Rounding the orange grove.

The stench of cow dung began filtering into her nostrils. The smell of safety! Gia didn't have a plan but bolted doors and little red buttons that summoned the police seemed a glorious place to start. They reached the far end of Lipica's paddock.

'He's coming!' Vuyo shrieked from just ahead of her.

Gia glimpsed over her shoulder, spotting Grizzly with heart-stopping suddenness. The monster was using the crutch she'd dropped for support. *The cheek of it!*

'Stop!' Grizzly called. 'Wait!'

As if! He had to be all flavours of nuts if he believed she'd do anything he said.

Vuyo took the corner at a hair-brained angle. His foot skated on loose bits of gravel. A hideous expression of horror ran across his face when his bandy legs buckled and he went down for the count.

Head over elbows over knees over head.

He missed the round metal bars of the cattle-grid by some freakish chance. 'Oouuch!' he yelled. Gravel ripped through his shorts and a bright red graze tore down the side of his kneecap.

Gia shot passed him. 'Get up!' she shouted, but he lay there, docile as a jellyfish. 'Vuyo?' She slammed on brakes, skidding, and the go-ped's motor roared to a halt, throttling smoke from its exhaust. Why wasn't Vuyo moving? How badly was he hurt? What if he was…? Gia froze. *No!* It wouldn't happen to her again. *Not twice in one lifetime.* 'Vuyo! Vuyo!' Gia gulped away the knot swelling in her throat. She couldn't afford to let fear in. Not now. She checked on Grizzly's progress.

His clothes were drenched. He moved with a limp, but with the span of his stride, time wasn't their friend. And judging by his expression, the maniac didn't intend fooling around.

'Help! Heeeeelp! Heeeeelp!' Gia screamed on the off-chance of fooling Grizzly into believing someone was up at the house. Just because *they* knew her dad was out didn't mean that he did.

The world remained silent save for the odd plop. Bitter wind nipped at her arms, its frosty teeth reminding her she had nothing but her wits to rely on. She needed a plan, a rock — anything. Gia took a quick look around. Her breath came in quick gasps, filling her lungs with an icy chill. Now what? She'd never considered herself a fighter, but after that unfortunate incident with her classmate, she knew a roaring warrior lived somewhere deep inside. All she had to do was find her… Somehow.

Heart giving a hop, skip and jump, Gia let the go-ped fall. She turned, squaring up to the monster behind them. Something inside her hardened like droplets of wax.

Grizzly was taller than expected but she'd underestimated her element of surprise fused with the power of girly spite. Partially out of instinct and partially out of wanting to teach him a lesson, Gia lifted her crutch by the uprights. She took a giant leap towards him, landed on her good foot and brought it down onto what she hoped was the ankle of his injured leg.

It was all in the timing.

Grizzly roared and crouched instinctively to nurse the pain.

Gia rammed his shoulder with the crutch's support beam. *He started it!* Who did he think he was, anyway? What kind of man tortured children and injured their pets in their own home? And where were the bogeyman police when she needed them?

Grizzly staggered. If not for *her* crutch that steadied his balance, he would have keeled over.

'Get away from us!' Gia was so close to him now that she registered high cheekbones and milky skin with dark racoon circles beneath blazing-blue eyes. His eyelids had bloated in their sockets and he looked exhausted. No doubt the effects of a bee colony committing suicide on his face. And despite knowing in her heart that it was so-very-wrong, a subtle sense of smugness that felt so, so, satisfying crept through her.

It didn't take long for karma to boomerang. It's what she got for rejoicing at the suffering of others, Gia grasped that fact right off the bat. As if the world had paused, her heart slammed against her ribcage when her gaze fell upon a dot of girly pink nail polish painted onto the crutch that Grizzly held.

He's got the crutch with the scroll!

Two things happened. Vuyo groaned, he sat up swirling somewhat and the sound of boots crunching gravel spoke of someone approaching from the side. Gia spun towards the sound and her eyes widened.

Elias had her dad's tranquilliser dart gun aimed at Grizzly's chest. He stepped around the corner of the Lipica's split-pole enclosure in his steady, controlled manner.

'Dad! Be careful, he has a gun!' Vuyo shrieked.

'He broke Nina's paw on purpose!' Gia howled.

'You little liar! That dog attacked me,' Grizzly had the gall to snarl. But he froze, staring at the dart gun while the drizzle turned radical; pelting suddenly as if determined to prove how flexible it could be.

'Move away from those children,' Elias said in that quiet, ghostly manner that stirred your insides.

'I'm looking for Samuel George Morgan.'

'Step. Away.'

Grizzly pulled his blunderbuss from the back of you-know-where and tossed it on the ground at Elias's feet. 'Recognise that? I understand Samuel has one just like it. I need to know where he got it from. Please, it's important.'

Elias never bothered looking at it. He persisted with a single-minded robot-like focus. But for the first time in Gia's life; he raised his voice. 'I won't ask you again!'

'They'll come for him.' Grizzly's eyes narrowed. 'His life could-'

Elias pulled back the spring of the dart gun.

Gia heard it catch. 'Wait! Who will come? Tell us what you know.'

'He's playing us, Gia. It's a tactic,' Vuyo crooned.

And as if proving Vuyo's point, Grizzly dropped like a sack. He pulled his arms to his chest. Hugging her crutch, he rolled himself below the split-pole structure of their horse paddock. It was such an unexpected thing for a grownup to do that Gia stepped towards the fence, confounded.

Lipica neighed, then reared, kicking her front legs into the air. Gia registered the galloping of hooves. Something that was heard and felt. Next thing, Lipica soared over the fence with Grizzly on her back and gripping fists of her white Lipizzaner mane, still clutching Gia's crutch

'Shoot him! Dad! Shoot!' Vuyo ordered.

'Lipica!' Gia yelled, watching the drama as if it were someone else's life. Which is why she couldn't blame Elias for doing the same. They stood idly by, gaping, as Lipica flew down the road. Her mother's horse galloped at such a speed that at times, all four of her limbs were in the air.

Chapter 12:

Hunter Scott

Gia's foot was back to looking like a bruised banana.

Her dad operated on Nina's leg while she sat on the floor of his surgery so that Jinja could snuggle on her lap. Her puppy's little body whimpered so much, it just about made *her* teeth rattle. Gia blubbered and snorted until Vuyo's hanky was sodden and she ended up holding deep, long breaths, trying to cure herself of the hiccups.

Vuyo tried to comfort her, but he didn't fare very well, so Tammy took over. She put Gia's moonboot in front of the oven to dry, fed her a pain pill and rubbed Vuyo's grazes with red antiseptic, making them look twice as large. Then she gave each of them a shoulder to howl on while scraping out their bee stingers with a piece of gauze.

Conflicting loyalties twisted Gia's insides. What if Grizzly had been telling the truth and Vuyo was wrong? Could someone have come for Oupie and taken him? If that was true, wouldn't they have asked for something by now? Also, his sentence starting with, *'You have the same-'* baffled her. What had Grizzly been about to say? Clothes? Crutch? Hair? It seemed weird. The business of Oupie's puzzle was gathering ever more pieces, and the black slug of failure was certain she couldn't guess which piece came next, only that she'd lost the most important one. How on earth was she going to find the scroll? She had no idea who Grizzly was. Or where! How could she spend her day looking for him when she was meant to be searching for Oupie?

'Let's give Nina a chance to sleep it off, shall we?' Gia's dad proposed some three hours later. He snapped off his surgical gloves and caught Gia by surprise by sweeping her into his arms and squeezing her so hard that she worried her ribs might crack. But she loved it. It made her insides unfurl a bit. She buried her face in the dent between his neck and shoulder and held on tight.

For the second time in as many days, Gia found Detective Steele parked in Oupie's study. Except that now, she sat on the leather couch leaning against a comfy pot-belly cushion, picking bits of skin from around her fingernails. Instead of that wonderful scent of Oupie's tobacco, Gia got a whiff of Detective Steele's head-on collision with an aftershave bottle. She watched him grunt his way through a one-sided, bent-neck telephone conversation while his fluffed-up eyebrows looked as if they were reaching for his hair.

Grizzly's blunderbuss lay on the desk, Tammy sat on the couch's armrest, patting down her elegant lime-green dress while Gia's dad leaned against the gun-case and Elias stood to attention at the door.

'Let's run through it again,' Detective Steel began once he'd ended his call. 'What were you doing down by the river?'

'Teaching Gia to swim,' Vuyo lied.

'In the rain?'

'It wasn't raining when we set out.' Vuyo shrugged.

'What was he doing by our river?' Tammy goaded. Her hands shook and Gia sensed her struggling with anger management. 'Was that someone from your search team you were speaking to on the phone? What did they say?'

Detective Steele snubbed her. He turned his face towards Gia, addressing her directly. 'What happened down there?'

'He pulled a gun on us.'

'You emptied a beehive on his head.'

'Because he pulled a gun on us!' Vuyo flipped his palms to the heavens, stretching his don't-you-get-it eyeballs.

'But only after you set your dog on him?'

'No, we never. Nina has a mind of her own!' Gia protested. She couldn't believe the day she was having. Not a predicament she'd considered possible. And there, at Polymead Grove. The country was where folks came to escape crime. Didn't he know that?

'She smelled a rat,' Tammy rattled like a sabre. 'And don't you dare blame them for this! I won't stand for it.'

'We found this.' Detective Steele placed a smudgy airline ticket on the desk. 'It seems the grizzly faced man has a name — Hunter Scott. He flew to Cape Town from Scotland shortly before Samuel's death, which explains the accent.' Detective Steele knitted his hairy knuckles together, and folding them over his curved belly. He leaned back in Oupie's chair before nudging his chin towards the blunderbuss. 'For the record, that gun isn't loaded. By the look of it, it's never fired a bullet.'

Gia shot Vuyo a befuddled glance, floored by the guessing game she'd fallen into.

'Why threaten them with it then?' Tammy's face appeared drenched in confusion.

Detective Steele rolled his shoulders. He leaned to the side and clicked the locks on a briefcase. 'There's been a development,' he declared, like it was a bad thing. 'We raided the containers of Worldwide Valuations Incorporated late last night and found this.' He plucked yet another blunderbuss from his case, putting it on the desk.

'That must be the gun they stole from my mom.' Vuyo deduced.

'Mmm. Seems likely because it has your mom's fingerprints all over it.'

'Do you think Hunter Scott's working for the Sanderson brothers?' Vuyo pried.

'I don't think he is,' Gia's dad murmured.

'Why not?' Tammy wanted to know.

'Because the Sanderson's went to tremendous effort to steal Samuel's weapon, then denied having it. Hunter Scott discarded the gun he had, no matter its value. I'd say their objectives aren't aligned.'

'I haven't been able to establish a link between them yet, Mrs Goodman. Not that there isn't one, though. What I'm saying is, we haven't really had time to look.' Detective Steele got up and packed both guns into his briefcase. 'I think it's prudent for me to leave my officers on patrol for a few days, just until we sort this out. I don't want anyone walking around here alone. Travel in pairs. No monkey business. No cowboy stuff. And I'd suggest that all of you stay together. Doesn't matter which house.'

'We're prisoners?' Tammy shrivelled her nose into a prune.

'Mrs Goodman.' Detective Steele sighed, sluggish on the exhale as if she'd pinched his last nerve. 'If you prefer, we could consider moving you elsewhere.'

'I'm not leaving my home!'

Detective Steele snorted, shook his head sadly and with a hint of condescension said, 'I don't think you've quite grasped the essence of what Gabriel Lance was implying.'

'Explain it to me then!' Tammy baulked.

'Hunter Scott wanted to know where Samuel got his guns from, he never asked where they were.'

'So?'

'Soooo, Samuel Morgan's shotguns aren't what Hunter Scott was looking for.' Detective Steele ran his eyes towards the police officer standing at the door and gave a subtle nod. The man strode from the room and returned seconds later with Gia's mud-covered crutch and Vuyo's waterlogged backpack.

Gia's heart skipped a double-beat. She sensed her left eyelid twitch when she spotted that the spongy bit of her armrest wasn't as flush as she'd left it. Had someone tampered with it? Who? Grizzly, or the police? She craved with every inch of her being to skip across the room and rip off the sponge so she could check on Oupie's secret. As it was, Detective Steel's gaze seemed as sharp as pins. Gia swallowed a lump that had swelled in her throat. She dressed up in her best poker face and slotted in beside him as he made his way to the door. 'Did you find any sign of Grizz... I mean, Hunter Scott?' Gia enquired.

'No! But we found the mare. I believe she belongs to you?' Detective Steele smiled. 'Stunning creature, if I may say so. There's something majestic about a white horse, isn't there?'

Gia returned his smile. 'She's a Lipizzaner.'

'I don't know what that means.'

'They're born black and lighten with age. And each of them can be traced back to eight stallions.'

'Ah.' A slight smile played on Detective Steele's lips.

'My mom named her Lipica after the original stud in Slovenia because my dad took her there on their honeymoon. She said it was one of her best days.'

Detective Steele bobbed his head and on her way through the door, Gia slurped up her crutch as indifferently as she dared.

'Want me to hose that down?' Her dad asked, putting a hand on the crutch's armrest.

'Oh… um…' Gia's mind ran the roller-coaster. 'I'm going to take a shower, I'll just stick it in there with me.'

Her dad pursed his lips and raked his fringe back. 'I'm going to give Lipica a quick squizz, then. Make sure she isn't hurt.' Their eyes met, and she sensed the heaviness in his heart. She understood the torment that trotted around him regarding her mother's horse. Hatred and anger because of the accident she'd caused and yet, a somewhat haunting desperation to ensure Lipica was well cared. Because, above all others, it's the animal her mother had loved — idolised. The last thing either of them wanted was to disappoint her mom. Even in death.

In the refuge of her bedroom, Gia ripped the spongy bit from the armrest of her crutch with one hand and held thumbs with the other, shoulders rigid. 'Yes!' She punched the air, hardly able to believe her luck as the scroll's tube popped out of its hidey-hole.

Vuyo paid her no heed. He turned his rucksack upside-down and shook it like a sheet. The key, the photographs of Oupie's guns, torch, spare batteries, an apple, a box of candles and a box of matches sprayed across her bedroom.

He looked up, alarmed. 'The riddle. It's gone, Gia.'

Chapter 13:

Family crest

Elias returned in the pouring rain, opening the door for Bongi and a chill of icy air. He closed their umbrellas, stamped out his boots, and handed Tammy overnight bags with a quick gesture for Vuyo to fetch the rest of their horde.

Bongi seemed unable to stop herself from humming a slow, methodical tune. She nursed a glass of sherry, burned citrus incense, then tapped, tapped her way through the house, blowing wafts of its smoke into every room. A police officer stood watching her through the window, worry lines on his brow as if thinking her actions might or might not be some kind of voodoo chant, Gia thought. *Not creepy at all.*

Tammy tried to cheer everyone up by roping them into helping her make pizza and chocolate mousse. When Jinja began begging for scraps, Gia decided that things were on the up and up.

Vuyo keeled over on the couch half-way through their movie. No doubt passed out from the leaves Bongi had crushed into their tea. Gia watched him snoring down trees. He looked different with his hair loose. Older. Fiercer. Maybe handsome.

The tea's relaxing qualities had a different effect on her. She lit a candle and lay on the couch watching wax roll off the candle's edge, dribbling down its side — something Oupie used to do. She missed him like a lost limb. He was just an old man, but he knew how to get along with a kid. Things like howling at the moon, searching for fairies, walks in the rain, ice cream with toppings and meals without vegetables.

Jinja snuck onto the couch beside her, one strategic paw at a time. She licked Gia's cheeks while the loud bell of longing chimed away inside her. She was kind that way. Besides, there were few things in life as comforting as a puppy's tongue. Gia whittled the time away by listening to the grownups play a ferocious game of scramble. She tried to think of something snappy to say to when she came face-to-face with Oupie again. Something about the idea calmed her. Then she remembered the lost riddle, an empty plateau, a sinking ship and the fact that they'd run out of clues, not to mention Hunter Scott's words of warning. Her entire being wanted answers and more and more it looked as if using the scroll was the way to get them. Somehow, they had to get it to show them where Oupie was. She was convinced it could.

Eventually, the grownups retired to their rooms, but Gia knew she wouldn't sleep, so she strolled to the kitchen to make hot chocolate. She stared through the window at slanting rain. Droplets clung to windowpanes as if trying to break in. She adored the way it gurgled through waterspouts, and remembered how, on rainy days, Oupie sat in front of a rip-roaring fire with a tot of whisky while she nursed a smouldering stick of sweet-smelling marshmallows. He'd rub the scar on his forearm and remind her that winter couldn't reign forever, even though he looked as if he wished that it would. Gia longed to sit on his lap tying nautical knots while he rambled on about Pop being a sea-creature. How he swam every morning come rain, hurricane or shine. And how he'd stay in the water until his fingers became wrinkly as if it were his sacred ritual.

The kettle spluttered and spat.

Gia stirred water into the chocolate powder, fetched her laptop and took it into the lounge. She squeezed herself back onto the couch between Jinja and Vuyo and settled into blowing into her mug while mulling over her day.

Vuyo gave a startled snort and came awake groggily. He propped his chest up when he saw Gia was awake, wiping the sleep from his eyes. 'What are you doing?' he croaked.

She leaned over, handed him her hot chocolate and hit him with, 'I've been thinking. How would Oupie know that twelve of those blunderbuss guns exist?'

Vuyo yawned.

Jinja put her chin on his lap, then bounced up and gave his face a glorious wet lick.

'Yuk!' Vuyo pushed her away with an acidic look and tried rubbing himself clean with his pyjama sleeve. He downed Gia's chocolate, straightened his hair, then examined Gia's face, blinking ponderously. 'He must have discovered it — researched the emblems, maybe?'

Gia squinted at him thoughtfully before tapping her laptop's screen. 'Which is what I thought we should do.'

'Now?'

Gia shot him her sulky-surly look.

'Might as well.' Vuyo stifled another yawn. 'Start by looking for the family crest.'

Gia typed into the search bar: FAMILY CRESTS.

There were hundreds. At least half the families on the planet had one.

Vuyo wrestled Detective Steele's photographs from his backpack. He jumped up, rushed off and came back with Oupie's magnifying glass before buckling down to assess the image. 'Gia.' He looked up, breathless. 'The family crest is a dragon. That must be why there's one on the gun.'

Gia scrutinised the page. Into Google's search bar she typed: FAMILY CRESTS WITH DRAGONS.

The list was shorter. They trawled through them, compared them inch by inch to the markings on Oupie's gun. In the end, they found two maybe-maybe-nots. It was harder to compare them than she'd hoped because the gun was metal, its emblems embossed silver, whereas images on the internet were bright and coloured in.

'It's either… House of Morgan. That's Oupie's surname! I didn't know his family crest was a dragon. It could explain the dragon on the gate. Hang on… the dragon from House of Canteridge looks the same to me,' Vuyo decided.

'Morgan means sea dweller!' Gia practically shrieked.

'The ship!'

'It fits. Listen to this. The wealthiest Morgans from the nineteen-sixty era owned a sugar plantation and a pet food company on the Natal coast. It all still exists. And…

Canteridge...' Gia tapped away at the keyboard with her index fingers. 'Um... there was an Earl of Canteridge.'

'A noble?'

'I guess so if he has a title.' Gia shrugged.

'Then he also fits because you said that nobles sometimes replaced the emblem used for country of origin with the number of their ship.'

'He's dead though.' Gia pointed at the distinguished gentleman with pulled back shoulders, twirled moustache and lofty nose who had popped up on her screen.

'Doesn't matter. We'll follow both leads until we have a reason to drop either of them.'

Gia bobbed her agreement. It felt like a clue, even though it wasn't much of one. 'I suppose the next thing to do is find out if either of these families owned a ship that was numbered V-double-zero-seven. Once we know that, we'll know who owned the guns. They're what started this mess, so they've got to be connected to things somehow.'

'As far as I know, we can only trace ship ownership through the National Archives.' Vuyo twisted his mouth to the side.

'One problem with that.'

'Just one?'

'Your mom won't let us go into Cape Town on our own. You know she won't.'

'Unless...' Vuyo's breath caught, his back straightened. 'Unless it was my birthday and the only alternative was us being locked up here.'

Gia dropped her jaw, giving him her you're-so-brilliant silent gape.

'You know how big my mom is on birthday celebrations.'

'And Oupie *always* took us into Cape Town for ice cream on our birthdays. So asking her wouldn't even be weird. The worst she can do is say no or insist on tagging along, right?'

'Absolute worst.' Vuyo flicked his eyes in a cocky manner. 'Soooo... it's a date?'

Gia recognised the trap she'd fallen into. 'That's not what I said.'

'Is it what you meant?'

'If it's what you want.'

'Is it what *you* want?' Vuyo asked with a shy smile and a sidelong glance.

Gia couldn't say why her heart was beating against her ribs. 'Would I have to wear a dress?'

'Do you own a dress?' Vuyo looked startled.

'No, I don't think so.'

She surprised a chuckle out of him. 'I like the way you usually dress. It's cool.' Vuyo flashed a big goofy grin just as the grandfather clock chimed ten 'o clock.

***

'Gia!'

Gia groaned. It was demon dark and the rain still rumbled.

Vuyo rolled her back and forth, flicked her lamp on and off. 'Gia! Wake up! Look at my birthday present.'

Gia turned over and Vuyo plonked himself onto her bed, stifling a giggle when Nina got stuck into licking his face as if he'd escaped from her food bowl. She could have sworn Vuyo almost barfed. 'What's the time?'

'Daytime.'

'Wet the bed?'

'What's Nina doing on your bed?' Vuyo grumped.

'She's sick. I'm nursing her. It's good to practise for if I become a vet.' Gia pointed out the bandage around Nina's foreleg. She thought it best not to mention that her dad fetching Nina from his surgery had everything to do with the fact that he'd rushed into her room because she'd come awake screaming. He'd even hugged her again. A sure sign of how desperate he was becoming. Gia had pretended to fall asleep, so he'd leave. It wasn't fair on him, sitting there on her couch staring at her with his long face of hopelessness.

'Dogs don't belong on furniture, Gia.' Vuyo's black eyes glared their disapproval. 'You could catch a disease.'

'Happy birthday, old man.'

80

'You're older than me.'

'And wiser.' Gia nodded. 'Why did you wake me up so early, I've only just fallen asleep?' Gia switched on the light and neatened Vuyo's tousled ponytail.

'My dad said I can have the afternoon off if I milk the cows in his place this morning. And I'm going to need it off because…' Vuyo jumped up and threw his arms wide. 'Ta-da! We're going into town!'

'What?' Gia scowled. 'Your mom said yes? No way, you're kidding.'

'Nope.' Vuyo rolled his eyes, shook his head.

'Did you mention we wanted to go alone?'

'Yup.'

'And you're sure she understood you?'

'I made sure of it! We got lucky because your dad was there. He said that whatever Hunter's looking for, he's looking for it on the farm, so it should be okay. My dad agreed. Then your dad said that he's going back to Oupie's attorney on account of them not finishing what they started yesterday. Him having had to rush home and all that. So he sees no reason we can't tag along. I told them you wanted to stick with tradition and take me for ice cream because that's what Oupie always did for our birthdays. My mom cried.'

Gia slapped a hand over her mouth. So. Many. Levels. Of. Wrong.

'Then she bounced back. She gave us a three-hour time limit. *She* says if we dare leave that ice cream parlour, we won't live to see another sundown. My dad says we better believe it.'

Gia did believe. Her heart sank. 'So we're… just going for ice cream, then?'

'Nah, don't worry. I suggested the ice cream parlour closest to the archives.' Vuyo purred from the pleasure of his grand plan.

'Um… who are you and what have you done with Vuyo?' So stunned was she that her hand still covered her mouth. It suddenly felt as if her lies were so trivial and unimpressive compared to Vuyo's.

Vuyo threw a hand across his waist and bowed. 'You're welcome.' He smirked, looking guilty as sin. 'But no camping. My mom refused to budge on that. And your dad backed her up. Oh, kumbaya,' Vuyo jeered when he noticed her shock finally. 'It's not as if their angel wings are growing heavy either.'

'What? What do you mean?'

Vuyo glanced round. He stepped forward, hunching over the bed. 'Have you taken a look at the guards out there?'

'The police officers?'

'That's just it. There's no way they're police officers. Last night, yes, but not anymore.' Vuyo dropped the bomb.

Gia's eyes widened. 'What are they, then?'

'Those are private security guards, Gia. Their uniforms are wrong, their weapons are different, their mannerisms. Everything. Something and I don't know what, but something about this doesn't gel.' And before Gia had time to compute, Vuyo shoved his gift in her face. 'Look what I got.'

'No way! A cellphone!' Gia snatched the shiny gadget from his grasp. 'I thought we couldn't have them until we're thirteen.'

'We couldn't. But after yesterday, my mom wants me to be able to contact her or the police if something like that ever happens again. She got a delivery service to bring it through. They left it with a guard on the bridge. It's when he brought it to the house that I noticed their uniforms had changed.' Vuyo puffed out his chest and handed her an oh-so-neatly wrapped box. 'I got you something too.'

'You're not supposed to bring me presents on your birthday, you crumpet,' Gia murmured while her mind visited a galaxy far away. What had Detective Steele learned between last night and this morning that made him believe they needed private security guards? Should she be worried?

'Open it. Remember that secret I've been keeping?'

It was her mom's diamond bracelet, the one she'd lost.

'I spent *days* looking for it when you wouldn't come out of your room after the accident,' Vuyo explained. 'That's how my bike ended up in the river. I thought if I found it, it might cheer you up because I know how much it means to you but… then the police began whispering about an autopsy.' Vuyo shrugged. 'So now I'm giving it to you today.'

Gia stared, misty-eyed. The thoughtfulness of Vuyo's gesture touched her to the core, and she hardly knew how to respond.

He tapped his watch. 'Now hurry. Get up! Get dressed before they change their minds. Your dad wants to leave at eight,' he said and gave her a quick surprise-peck on the cheek, which made them both look away.

Chapter 14:

The Seeing Scroll

Gia pulled on a yellow, pink and purple paisley patterned gipsy pants and because she wanted to cover the lumpy bee stings on her arms, she wore her jean jacket. She touched up her fingernails, painted each toenail different colours, and even spent five minutes brushing her hair pretending to be a lady.

On her way to the kitchen, she noticed Bongi's bedroom door was ajar. She crept up to it.

'Bongi's awake, Chile,' Bongi's seductive voice drawled.

'How do you do that?' Gia laughed and crossed the carpet to hug her, leaving her crutches at the door so they wouldn't get in Bongi's way. They reserved this guest room for Bongi. She slept over often and knew the layout so it made things easier, but Gia knew Bongi would cope anywhere. She had a knack for things, maybe because she'd almost always been blind with the last of her limited eyesight being lost to the measles at thirteen.

The smell of vanilla incense thickened the air. A horde of battery-operated candles crammed onto an Oregon table that sat low to the ground crafted a muted glow that made Bongi's guest bedroom sort-of inviting. She used to use real ones. But Tammy wouldn't allow it anymore, not since Bongi had set a curtain alight.

King Proteas spruced up a plush mantelpiece. On the left of Bongi's bed sat an almond leather couch that looked as if no one had ever used it. Bongi had swept its sea of randomly sized mismatched cushions onto the floor where they now gathered around the Oregon table. At the far end of the room was an en-suite bathroom. From where Gia stood, she heard the trickle of a tap.

On the right of the bed, Bongi rested in a lush, cherry bonbon rocking chair that pitched rhythmically back and forth. She was still in her dressing gown and minding a pulled back curtain in front of an open window, despite sporadic rain. Outside, an owl called for its mate. A pale gleam of sunrise flickered across Bongi's face and Hex, Bongi's fluffy, coal-black cat, napped on the chair's backrest as if he was part of the décor.

Gia stepped into the path of the cool air and breathed it in, startling at her reflection in the window. 'I'm making a pot of coffee. Would you like some, Bongi?'

Bongi lay a beaded arm across her knee, palm facing upwards. She kept rocking.

Gia knew what it was — an invitation. She checked her watch. The temptation was too much, of course. Limping around the Oregon table, she threw her arms round Bongi's shoulders and hugged her so hard that even the beads around her neck rustled with pleasure. She settled Hex into Bongi's lap and plonked herself, cross-legged, on a cushion at Bongi's feet. Then Gia placed her hand in Bongi's, palm down. It was soft, warm and cosy.

A familiar look of concentration crossed Bongi's face.

A minute passed.

Three.

Silence, save for a dripping tap and purring cat.

'You've had a... different week, yes?' Bongi drawled.

'Yes.'

'Learned something new?'

'Yes,' Gia whispered, careful now.

With her fingertips, Bongi traced the lines on Gia's palm at a worm's pace. 'You know what Elias would say if he catches us now,' Gia teased. But she was enchanted, hooked. There was something about Bongi's manner that enthralled her.

'Mmm,' Bongi hummed, looking pleased. 'Don't mess with the spirits, just now they mess with you?'

They shared a nice long giggle.

Bongi stroked Hex's forehead. A gesture that flattened his ears and stretched the skin on his head until it looked as if his eyes had popped forward. 'Bongi needs her book, Chile.'

'Book?'

'I only brought one.' Bongi gestured towards a frothy, lace-covered book that lay on the bedside cabinet.

An odd request for a blind person, Gia thought, and a hot flush stole into her cheeks as her gut rebuked her. A shame that increased tenfold when she balanced the book on Bongi's lap and realised it was in Braille and she was the fairy who couldn't read it.

'Bongi's ready for your question, Chile.'

Gia opened her mouth, closed it. She did so like her. 'Um… has anyone ever asked you to keep a secret, Bongi?'

A bemused smile lit the corner of Bongi's lips. She never replied.

'Oh… um… and if you found out that it could be a dangerous secret? Would you say something, then?'

'If it's not my secret to tell, Chile, then it's not my secret to tell.'

'Oh.' Gia stared at the flickers of daylight for a time. 'Um…' She cleared her throat. 'You used to be a fortune teller, didn't you, Bongi?'

'Used to be? Noooo. It's a gift, Chile. It lives inside Bongi the same way that music lives inside you.'

'But, does being able to read someone's fortune mean you believe in… magic?'

Bongi's milky gaze shifted towards the window, her mouth crimped in the corners. 'You're referring to the legends, yes?'

'Could any of them be true?'

'Some people say.'

'What do those people say about the artefacts you spoke of?'

'I'm not a crystal ball, Chile. Ask me what you want to know.'

Gia chuckled at Bongi's manner. It was now or never, she decided. She wouldn't be gifted another perfect opportunity. 'Are there any artefacts you know of that would explain… seeing strange things? Visions of sorts?'

'Ah.' Bongi's forehead dipped into a rare frown. She whistled through her teeth on the intake of breath.

'What? Do you know something?' Gia clenched her fist.

'Bongi knows many things, yes.' Bongi leaned forward, her gaze still watching the window. 'Tell me, Chile. These visions, are they only seen or can they also be felt?'

Gia held her tongue, but Bongi opened her book to the first page. Using both hands, her fingertips dribbled along a series of dots that Gia assumed was an index because it didn't take long for Bongi to begin paging. She stopped about a quarter way into the book. When she spoke again, her tone gave Gia the heebie-jeebies. 'This thing of which you speak, it's a scroll, yes?'

Gia hesitated, and a little shiver ran across her shoulders.

'No?' Bongi raised an eyebrow.

Gia chewed her lip, her hand tracing the bone at the base of her neck. She wished Vuyo was here. She didn't know what to do. Bongi was harmless, though. She wouldn't tell anyone, would she?

'Yes?' Bongi prompted. 'It's important, Chile. No artefact is identical to another.'

'It could be a scroll.'

'Ancient parchment, yes?'

'Yes.'

'Chalky?'

'Very.'

'Small?'

'Tiny.'

Bongi pulled her nose up, cringing. Even Hex startled awake, looking troubled. 'Markings?'

'None.' Gia pleaded.

'This scroll, think, Chile. Does it roll itself closed?'

'You do know it!' Gia could have sworn the candles flickered, and the incense snuffed itself out.

Bongi rocked back and forth with minuscule movements. 'The Seeing Scroll. It's believed to be lost. Daaangerous magic.'

'Why? Dangerous how?'

'Why so many questions about an enchanted scroll, Chile?'

Gia grabbed Bongi's hands that had somehow turned cold as a bucket of ice. 'Tell me what you know! It's important, Bongi. And you have to keep it a secret. Swear it.'

'The Seeing Scroll is said to have a sense of place.' Bongi jogged her head and the bone-beads round her neck jingled. 'Oh, yes. It remembers the past and shows you what happened in a place. Some people say it shows the darkest and most dangerous of secrets.'

'Which people? And whose secrets?'

'Yeees, that's what they say. But beware, if the past is where you get comfortable, the past is where that scroll will make you stay.'

'It traps you there?' Gia's mouth went dry as toast.

'Stray too long where you don't belong and the world you're from could be forever gone.' Bongi turned her spooked face away from the window. 'Cursed that thing is.'

A chill marched into Gia's stomach. She gawped at Bongi with eyes she sensed had gone as wide as waffles. Everything she thought she knew spiralled away and her mind leapfrogged to a horror not previously imagined. What if Oupie was stuck in the scroll?

The idea was crazy.

Maybe Bongi was crazy.

Gia didn't get that sense from her, though. Never had.

What if Bongi was right? Oupie had survived the accident, there was no doubt in Gia's mind. Could the scroll be the reason for his disappearance? And the reason they hadn't heard from him? Or was it related to Hunter Scott's warning? Neither option made sense. Because if Oupie was in the scroll, it meant that someone else had hidden it in the desk after he'd used it. And someone else had sent the key that made them look.

Gia almost gasped aloud. She clapped her hands over her mouth in the nick of time. *Elias!* Could it be? What if that was why he'd explained where they'd gone wrong on the day they'd searched Oupie's study?

'How long is too long?' Gia squeaked.

'Ten blinks of the eye.'

'But… that's not long. Is there a way to break such a curse, Bongi?'

'Some people say.'

Relief surged through Gia's shaky heart. 'Which people? Do you mean the book?'

'Yes, Chile. The book. Ancient it is. A collaboration.'

'Does the book say how?'

'No. Oh, no. Only that it's never happened.'

The world seemed to slow. A horrid lump inflated in Gia's throat and her eyes went blurry.

Bongi grabbed her by the hand, her voice hoarse and for a just a second Gia imagined her gaze was focused. 'Are you imagining what I think you're imagining, Chile?'

Gia wrenched her hand free and hobbled from the room.

***

Gia wiped her eyes, trying to slow her breath and stop her hands trembling.

Could the scroll be cursed? The more she thought it through, the more absurd it seemed that Elias would have directed her towards something dangerous. He would have known she'd ask Vuyo for help, and he wouldn't risk his son's life. Unless, of course, Elias was in the dark about what the scroll did. Perhaps he hadn't tried using it? Also, if it had been peppermint she'd smelt in the cave behind the waterfall on that first day, it implied Elias had been there. Why would he give her a key to search a place where he'd already looked? And anyway, was it wise to believe something so horrid without a lick of validation?

By the time Gia reached the kitchen, the rain had stopped. The first thing she noticed was the black, unmarked vehicle with tinted windows parked in the driveway. From beneath her eyebrows, she scrutinised the guards loitering on the terrace, contemplating Vuyo's remarks. There were four of them, all dressed in black, with backs straight as pens and little wires running up their necks into earpieces. The colour of early morning cold burned through their cheeks. Was Vuyo's suspicion right? Did their parents know they weren't police officers? Surely Elias would have noticed a change, too?

It's because Gia watched them instead of what she did that the flour bag burst and spilt across the floor — true story. In her haste to slosh a mop through the mess, she'd neglected to rinse the water out of it. By the time her dad stood in the doorway with his hair sleek and gelled back, stubborn flour-glue leeched onto their chessboard floor.

'Coffee?' Gia chimed, putting a sparkle in her voice. She spent the next few seconds hoping her dad would at least notice Jinja pulling her four-legged weight and trying her level best to help lick the floor clean.

'Um… yes please.'

Gia scuttled across the flour-glue in her bare feet.

'What are you doing?' her dad ventured.

'Baking a cake.'

'For breakfast?'

'For Vuyo's breakfast. I thought I'd surprise him when he comes back from the barn.' She'd hoped to come in under the radar too, but that was yesterday's dream.

Her dad was abnormally dressed in suit pants, a dress shirt and a green tie. He chomped on his lip watching her crises unfold. Next thing he hopped, skipped and jumped the cleanest path to the mop in his navy blue socks that had pink kittens on them, and began scrubbing.

Gia spooned sugar into her dad's mug and stirred. Her heart swelled in her chest while she watched. He always wore what she bought him without complaining about the colour. And after what the world had put him through, the fact that he was so easily able to compose himself was a near miracle. She grasped that most dads would have thrown ten hissy fits by now. Gia delivered his coffee to the booth, swung round and hugged him.

'And now?'

'I love you, daddy. You're the best.'

'Ah,' he breathed, but she caught the buzz of contentment in his voice. 'Here.' He handed her a handful of bills. 'Don't let Vuyo pay for his ice cream. And… um… I've been contemplating surprising him too.'

'How? Vuyo *loves* surprises.'

'Well, maybe… if we played him a song or two later on?'

Gia yanked the sleeve of her jacket that seemed rather determined to crawl into the bowl and sneak a taste of her batter. 'Maybe,' she murmured, turned and toppled her cake mixture into the pre-buttered container. She licked her fingers, careful to avoid eye contact. She couldn't think of a worse idea. Perhaps it was an omen? Perhaps going to the archives wasn't such a brilliant plan after all.

She stepped up onto a chair and popped the cake mixture into the microwave mounted onto the wall. The timer began its countdown. One of the guards peered through the window, watching. Gia didn't get it. What exactly had convinced Detective Steele that the men on the porch were more suitable than his own guards? If they were in that much danger, why hadn't he said so? Why hadn't he barred them from leaving the farm? If not her dad's, whose payroll were they on? Because no way would he hire private guards and then let her loose in Cape Town. Not him. And why did their presence suddenly feel like a threat?

Four not-so-neatly wrapped gifts, one lopsided cake, a birthday song and two cups of coffee later they made their way to the rear of her dad's car. Two of the men-in-black followed her. One on each side while chattering into their mics.

Perhaps she was reading too much into things, but they didn't follow Vuyo.

Chapter 15:

National Archives

The valley looked different as it whizzed past the car window. Shrubs and apple trees blurred into one, and everything became a carpet of lush velvet. And yet, the shapes of the mountain and the gaps between them remained distinctive.

The family graveyard loomed large. A kilometre after that they approached a red rose garden bordering an immaculate lawn and a pair of fabulous, white columns that signalled the entrance to Vuyo's house. Gia rolled down the window and breathed the sweet smell of roses while relishing the way air moved over her skin as they cruised along. At the end of Vuyo's long winding driveway stood a tall, white-washed house with green window frames, green slanted roof and an upstairs terrace that watched the valley and a section of the river.

The drive into town took one dreary hour. Gia used it to yackity-yack about Bongi's sentiments, ensuring she kept her voice low.

'Those are secrets that we're seeing?' Vuyo's face grew ever more troubled until he'd scrunched his eyes into slits. 'Whose?'

'How must I know whose?'

'It's rubbish, Gia. There's no way a ship that size could crash without someone seeing it. Or parts of it. And anyway, why would it be a secret? Also, if Oupie's stuck in the scroll, it means that someone else sent the key.' Gia raised an eyebrow and Vuyo's face tightened. He clamped his lips, hissing through his teeth. 'I know what you're thinking, but it can't be my dad.'

'You *don't know* what I'm thinking.'

'My dad would look for Oupie himself! You know he would.'

Elias tapping the wall in Oupie's bedroom sprang into her mind and she sighed. 'I know nothing anymore. But that's what today's about, isn't it? Finding answers? Maybe we should give it a chance?'

'I'm sorry to say this, Gia. But… chance or no chance, let's hope Bongi's way-off the mark because I don't see how finding out who owned a ship that once carried a handful of guns will help us get anyone out of an enchanted scroll.' Vuyo squeezed her hand as if trying to transfer his warmth into it.

Vuyo had a point. Gia turned to stare through the window. As they approached Cape Town, the world morphed into a massive concrete jungle. Houses seemed smaller, meaner, squarer. Gia leaned her elbow against the window, chin in hand, watching the traffic crawl along.

Stop. Start. Stop. Start.

The first thing she heard when she climbed out of the car in the city centre, was hooters blaring. She watched people crowding on a common. Men in T-shirts, women in skirts. Crossing the road, she stared at swirling plastics, polystyrene mugs and cigarette butts. Not for the first time, she felt blessed to live on a farm.

The National Archive was a bland but majestic, brown-brick structure with high ceilings, delicately embossed cornices, long, grubby wooden windows and yellowing floors covered with an unimpressive layer of caked-on polish. Inside, it was so sparsely furnished that the thud, thump, thud, thump of Gia's crutches alternating with her shoe echoed with an air of spookiness as she made her way down the corridor.

People came and went through imposing green doors that stretched to twice the normal height, as if giants had walked the earth when the building was built. It gave Gia a sense of optimism because it made the place look every bit as old as the information she hoped to find.

She stood for a moment. It wasn't hard imagining grand balls, music, lah-di-dah dresses, and the Lords and Ladies that must have once graced these halls. She wondered if any of them still lived. Or had descendants. If they'd lived good lives.

Instead of combing through corridors of boxes as she'd expected, they wrote House of Morgan and Earl of Canteridge on an information sheet. They handed it in and were allocated a number. Then found themselves in a dingy waiting room that reeked of damp towels and mouldy bread.

'Don't touch anything, you'll catch your death,' Vuyo warned and dug his hands into his pockets.

A middle-aged man with dark, fluffy hair and the build of a box collected their request. He wore a light-blue shirt, black jacket, black scuffed shoes and a dull badge labelled *Administration Assistant*. Gia approved of his aftershave: half-musky-half-spicy. Not the sharp tang that Detective Steele had chosen.

'What's this for — school assignment?' Mister Box fished.

They both nodded at the option he'd provided.

'Name?'

'Gia Lance and Vuyo Goodman.'

'Lance?' Mister Box grunted. 'Not related to Gabriel Lance by any chance?' He poked an absent-minded thumb at the poster on the wall behind him while completing a sheet of paper.

The picture showed a fair-haired man seated at a piano in front of a jam-packed auditorium. *Master pianist in concert*, it read. And diagonally across the poster, in red ink, *Cancelled*.

Gia froze and concentrated on swallowing what felt like a bit of this morning's flour-glue that had congealed in her throat.

Mister Box's eyes narrowed and as if someone had flicked a switch, he gasped. 'Oh, my goodness. You're his daughter!'

'Um… my dad doesn't play anymore,' she said hastily, and her tummy tightened.

'Yes, but… you're the little girl who could play everything he could play by the time you turned five.'

A nerve in her eyelid twitched.

'If you don't mind, we're actually in a bit of a hurry,' Vuyo mumbled.

Mister Box stared and stared.

Vuyo cleared his throat. Loudly.

Mister Box glanced at Vuyo and Gia saw understanding catch. 'Oh… Uh…' He looked back at her, lowering his head, sympathetic now. 'Of course. He's still in mourning, then? I'm so sorry about your mother. I'll just be a minute,' he murmured and sauntered off.

'Thanks,' Gia whispered as he vanished through the door.

'It's bound to happen from time to time.'

'What I meant was, thanks for always being there.' On impulse, she threw her arms around Vuyo's neck and gave him a quick squeeze.

'There's nowhere I'd rather be,' Vuyo breathed into her ear.

Mister Box returned half-an-hour later, unrushed and humming. He pushed a trolley with a tray of tacky papers, which he spread across a table.

Gia rifled through them with a dreadful eagerness.

'There are plenty of ships registered to the House of Morgan, even today, but they're American,' Mister Box said. 'And their numbers start with M, not V like you said.'

Vuyo huffed in disappointment.

'I could only find one Earl of Canteridge, though.' The old man delivered a second box that threatened to split at its seams.

Gia risked lifting a page and read. 'The Earl was born in Scotland in nineteen-thirty-nine and set sail for the Cape of Storms in February nineteen-sixty-two.'

'Does that suit your timeline?' Mister Box enquired.

'We don't have one,' Gia explained. 'All we know is that the person we're looking for had something made and branded with the number of their ship. That's what we think, anyway.'

'I see.' Mister Box ran his tongue over his teeth. He dusted flakes of dandruff from his jacket before he continued. 'Well, this Earl inherited his ships from his father, so maybe his father had things branded. In which case your timeline could be different. Also, the Canteridge peerage was returned to the British Crown.' He delved into the box, drew out a page and squinted into the light. 'That happened around February nineteen-sixty-five. A year after he set sail, then.'

'What does that mean?' Vuyo puckered his brow.

'A peerage is a title. It's the reason he was an Earl,' Gia replied.

'Correct.' Mister Box smiled and his wrinkles creased into little spiderwebs. 'And if it was returned to the Crown, it means the Earl died without a rightful heir.'

Vuyo pursed his lips.

Mister Box seized another page from his pile and Gia got the impression that he was relishing the mystery. 'It says here that at the time of his passing the Earl of Canteridge co-owned three vessels with his mother, the Countess of Stafford: *Starlight* — S003, *Orion* — O004 and *Velox* — V007.'

Gia's heart skipped a beat. 'That's the one! That's the number on the customised item.'

'Pity.' Mister Box clicked his tongue as if he too was disappointed. 'This is the end of the road, I'm afraid. Access to the Earl's documents were sealed in…' He pulled a blue envelope from the pocket behind his *Administration Assistant* nametag, narrowed his eyes and recited, 'Nineteen-seventy-nine. That's fourteen years after he died.'

'Why? I mean… why bother if the Earl had been dead for so long?'

'Hard to say. It's not something I've seen before but…' Mister Box rolled his square, meaty shoulders. 'Something must have happened between the time of the Earl's passing and the sealing of these records. I don't think this can be done without a court order.'

'A legal process?' Vuyo puzzled.

'Mmm.'

'Then it's a dead-end.' Vuyo pulled a face and Gia sensed him struggling to mask his disappointment.

It didn't feel like a dead-end to her. They now knew that Oupie's guns had once belonged to the Earl of Canteridge. He or his father had them made. They hailed from Scotland, and they'd crossed the ocean on his ship called *Velox*. It seemed an incredible *co-ink-i-dink* that Hunter Scott had undertaken the exact journey, albeit on an aeroplane, the moment Oupie's or rather, the Earl's guns had surfaced. And yet, after coming all this way, Hunter had failed to display even a measly bit of interest in their current whereabouts. So why had he come? Gia was tempted to fall on the idea of the scroll but if she was being practical, nothing proved a link between the guns and the scroll. At least, not yet. She wanted to know more. She needed to. 'What about newspaper articles? Let's try them. They can't be sealed, can they?'

Mister Box beamed 'No. Once in print, always in print. You can never put a lid on a juicy story and the tabloids *love* reporting on nobles,' he slurred and nodded as if they had settled the matter. Mister Box pulled back his shoulders and flicked away a few more specks of dandruff. He tried looking down at Vuyo. Didn't work, Vuyo was taller than him. 'If you're serious about your research, it's worth taking a trip to the library and going through the microfilms of newspapers for that period.'

'Where's the library?' Gia bounced at the chance.

'That period spans fourteen years, Gia. We don't have time for that.' Vuyo shot her a look that could have fired cannons.

'We don't have to read everything,' Gia buzzed.

'Exactly.' Mister Box joined their squabble. 'Pick keywords, search for bits and bobs. You should be able to piece the story together. I bet you that none of the other kids doing this project will do that. You'll get bonus marks, I'm sure. What have you got to lose?'

Thank goodness Vuyo was quick on his feet and thinking sensibly too, because the next thing he babbled was, 'How far is the library?'

'Not far. It's your lucky day. Two blocks up.'

Chapter 16:

The library

Gia peered around the National Archive's entrance door.

A stream of folks with shopping bags marched along the pavement like troops of ants, a woman in clicking heels hailed a taxi and a ragged fellow begged with an outstretched cup. Next to him, a man with tight shoulders stood at a magazine stand perusing his options. He wore all black except for a grey, padded coat, and he kept glancing around as if waiting for someone.

Gia's heart gave an unsettling thud. He reminded her of the guards at the farm, but when he glanced towards them, his gaze fell away, disinterested. He selected a magazine and Gia caught sight of an odd tattoo across the back of his hand — a skull draped with an awesome cap.

'It's this way.' Vuyo gestured after searching the library's location on his cellphone. He got busy swaggering in his Superman shirt and lemon-yellow swimming trunks that she'd given him for his birthday. He pretended they weren't together, shielding his face with her best present of all, a cap that said, *Guilty!* Which had caused Elias to chuckle and bob his head in agreement.

A fair-haired man drove by and Gia ducked when her guilty conscience thought it recognised her dad. She used a long stripe of passengers standing at a bus stop as a shield. Peered back. The man looked nothing like her father; the beggar was still there and the fellow with the grey coat lingered over his magazine, paying them no heed.

You're getting paranoid! Why would anyone be following you? White noise, that's what her dad called it when he allowed insignificant things to distract his focus. She resolved to refocus on the Earl, his ship, and what it had to do with Oupie.

Unlike the National Archive, the library was extraordinarily inviting. The carpets were soft, the kiddie paintings stuck on the walls, bright and cheery. Lavender-scented furniture polish floated through the air, competing with that magnificent pong of old books.

'That one, Mommy! And that one. How many can I choose?' A little girl with gorgeous brown curls bounced.

'Shh!' Almost everyone else hissed.

The place became so quiet Gia imagined that she'd hear a feather flutter. A little deceptive, because it created an aura that encouraged them to take as much time as they needed. Something they couldn't do.

The crotchety looking librarian must have decided they oozed shifty vibes because she took one look at them and plodded over. 'Yes?'

'We'd like to see your microfilms of newspapers, please,' Gia murmured.

The woman smelled of strong coffee and freshly peeled oranges. She frog-marched them to the back corner of the adult section and gestured a skinny, bangled arm at towering drawers of immaculately numbered microfilms. 'They're filed in the sequence of year, month, day. You can search for a range of dates, and four words maximum. Put them back where you find them. Make sure your hands are clean. Pay now, please.' She stuck out her hand.

'Um, also,' Gia asked while paying. 'Do you perhaps know offhand where you keep your books on artefacts?'

'Fiction or non-fiction?'

'Magical artefacts.'

'The corner behind you,' the librarian barked and stomped her way towards a trolley stacked with shoulder-height piles of books. She began feeding them back onto shelves.

'Gosh, she's friendly.' Vuyo mumbled and sat, making the sound of a deflating tyre.

Gia understood the problem. The archive should have provided answers, not raised more questions and handed them a bunch of work. And yet, here they were, and on Vuyo's birthday to boot. It occurred to Gia how much Vuyo was prepared to sacrifice for her. But most of all, how blessed she was to call him her friend. 'Why don't you run as many searches as you can and just print everything while I see about the scroll. That way we can read them later and save time for the ice cream parlour so we can celebrate your birthday. What do you say?' she suggested, putting brightness in her voice.

Vuyo's face lit. He nodded, huddled over the keyboard and typed the words: *Canteridge, Stafford, Velox* and *V007* into the application's search bar. Gia turned and hobbled her way towards the corner the librarian had pointed at. She scoured the shelf.

Nothing notable.

The title of almost all the books was Artefacts of somewhere or other: Egypt, Greece, China, Africa. Her shoulders wilted. A mission-impossible task. She had no cooking-clue where the scroll originated. Scotland would be her best thumb suck. She skimmed the list of countries along the back of spines. Nothing that mentioned Scotland. But wedged into the corner, she discovered a blue cotton overlaid paperback. *Lost Artefacts*, it read.

Gia yanked it from the shelf and flipped to the content page, recalling how Bongi had mentioned that the Seeing Scroll was rumoured to have been lost. She ran her index finger down the list. A single scroll appeared — *The Banishing Scroll.*

Oh dear. The name grabbed her by the chest and her finger paused. It sounded like the actions of the scroll Bongi had described. Could she have confused the two? Gia skipped to the listed page number and in a moment of reckoning caught sight of the words.

Vanished from Scotland in the early 1900s.

Gia scanned the image. It looked like the one she had, she thought, and turned the page.

Curse of the Banishing Scroll:
What some would hide
This scroll would let you see,

And below that, a write-up: The Banishing Scroll is said to have a sense of place which is triggered by its sense of blood. Gia froze, fear knotting her stomach. What did a sense of blood mean? Revenge? That's what it sounded like? And why did a horrible hunch suggest that the Banishing Scroll and the Seeing Scroll were one-and-the-same, and that Bongi's theory wasn't far-fetched after all? Before she could digest the information, the main entrance door cracked open. Gia turned to look.

A man wearing a grey jacket entered. *Is that the fellow I saw outside the National Archive building?* He glanced left, right, and moved towards the librarian.

Gia lowered her head, turned to stand at an angle. She leaned over the printer, collecting their wad of printouts, pretending to scan through them while keeping an eye peeled to the stranger. Something about his manner pricked her radar. She didn't know why. Just a feeling. An uneasy one. She strained to listen.

He nodded as a way of greeting the librarian, muttered something inner-mouthed, and Gia got an image of a young, clean-shaven face. He flashed the librarian a card, held up his cellphone and tapped its screen.

In that split-second, Gia spied a tattoo on the back of his hand — a skull wearing a cap. The knot in her stomach twitched tighter. 'Vuyo,' she croaked.

The librarian gestured vaguely in their direction and Gia's heart flick-flacked. Could he be looking for them or was she still being paranoid? Perhaps Tammy had sent one of the guards to protect them? Not a risk she wanted to take, Gia decided. She shoved their printouts beneath her shirt and moved to use a bookshelf as a screen. 'Vuyo,' she hissed.

Vuyo looked up and Gia nudged her chin towards the counter. He blinked two ticks. 'Follow me.' He slipped from his seat and led her by the arm. They crept between shelves and crouched in their shadows, going still.

Mister Coat turned and made his way towards the microfilm machine, skimming a glance around.

They darted into the children's section.

Crouched.

Waited a second.

Ten.

He was looking for them! What did he want? Perhaps they should call her dad? Even while thinking about it, Gia knew they'd have to escape first. She followed Vuyo along a short wooden passage that creaked and cracked. She froze and unfroze, making her way towards a fire-escape exit that led to who-knew-where. She reached another carpet and began limp-running. Vuyo moved faster and faster and Gia hopped along, determined not to lag.

She went past flushing toilets.

A kitchen.

Mister Coat stepped into the passage.

'Run!' Gia cried.

Vuyo sprinted for the fire-escape door. Pushed.

Nothing.

He shoulder barged it.

Gia reached him and they rammed the door with their collective weight. With a low cow-like groan, it gave. Vuyo half-tossed Gia through the opening, tipping her into a shock of sunlight and a rush of warm air that swirled between masses of people, gassy hissing of a truck's brakes, blaring hooters and the tap-tap-tapping of traffic lights cautioning the blind.

Now what? Should they run? Where to? What about hide? Mister Coat wouldn't attack a child in front of witnesses, surely? Perhaps staying in a public place was safer?

Gia heard voices hum. Her senses flooded with a stench of greasy, fast-food odours and the distinct feeling that everyone's eyes were trained on her.

'Let's go in there!' Vuyo pointed at a bustling cluster of craft market stalls littering the pavement across the street at the end of the block.

They zipped past a church.

Jaywalked across a cobble stone intersection.

Gia glanced back, balling her hands into fists. Just then Mister Coat sprang into the air, looking around, his icy eyes fixed on her.

He began running. She dodged in between trestle-table stalls and came into a square where a spouting-dolphin fountain hissed while barterers shrieked their offers and small spinning fans kept flies at bay.

Why was he chasing them? What did he want? Was he the *"they"* that Hunter Scott had been referring to? He couldn't be one of their guards. It came to her in a flash because Tammy wouldn't have hesitated to lord his presence over them.

Again, Gia peeked over her shoulder and again she noticed Mister Coat. Close. He surged through the crowd and clamped a hand on her shoulder, making her yelp. She caught a whiff of alcohol, a fragrance she recognised because there was a time after her mom died that her dad's best friend was the spirit in a bottle.

'Help! Vuyo!' Gia tried twisting away. She stumbled into a stall, toppling small, brightly painted wooden elephants onto their sides. Their little eyes stared up at her as if in disapproval. Gia changed direction. Her stupid crutch wedged into a stupid rut. It plucked free from her grasp and fell. She staggered, almost rectified, but trod on it at the last minute. The plastic of her moonboot skated on the wood as if she'd stepped on glass. The spongy bit softening the armrest brought her boot to an abrupt halt.

It held for a second.

Then gave.

Thud!

Gia landed on a bulging cobble, hissing on the intake of breath. The scroll's tube tinkled from its hidey-hole. It rolled across the ground and settled into a rut much like a discarded cigarette stub. Gia clutched for it, her knees scraping stone.

Mister Coat was closer. He lunged.

A sideswipe movement came across him like a stage curtain. There was a moment of utter bewilderment when someone dive-tackled Mister Coat and Gia spied grown men sprawling on the ground like cubs entangled in not-so-playful banter.

Fists and feet thrashed.

A head popped out of the fistfight. An elbow smacked it on the nose.

The planet swopped cogs, slowing to a sloth's pace.

Gia's jaw fell because she recognised their saviour.
Hunter Scott.

Chapter 17:

Finders Keepers

They never waited for him to explain.

Following a map on Vuyo's cellphone, they weaved between alleys, snuck through buildings and used back streets until they ducked into the ice cream parlour.

Vuyo stood at the entrance, watching the shadows.

The air conditioner was set to freezing. Gia wasn't sure if that's why her spine quivered and her skin bristled or if it was just plain fear. She focused on trying to stop her heart from rattling her ribcage, but her thoughts kept scattering. 'I don't get it. Why would Hunter help us?' Gia said in a voice so small it was swallowed by the throng of teenage boys who invaded the shop. One of them bumped her, jarring her back to her surroundings.

The place was teeming with moms and kids of all shapes and sizes, many of whom were their age. Gia leaned against the wall. She rubbed her arms, watching the teenagers gather in the centre of the parlour. They formed a circle and began singing Happy Birthday to their tallest recruit.

'Perfect timing. We'll be safe with them here,' Vuyo decided. 'Let's act as if we're part of their crowd. But we'll sit by the fire-escape and make sure that no one can see your moonboot from the door, just in case.'

Gia nodded, marvelling at how calm Vuyo seemed. Their parents had only let them come because they were certain that whatever Hunter had been searching for was on the farm. Mister Coat's attack proved otherwise. And judging by the way he'd lunged for the scroll — he'd recognised it. It's what he was after, him and Hunter Scott. It was the most logical explanation because it's the only thing they carried aside from a couple of bucks. Which implied there was some kind of link between the guns and the scroll and therefore, the Earl, the plateau and his ship. She couldn't reason it any other way.

Vuyo took her hand and got busy squeezing through the crowd of kids, making his way towards the counter. They had five ice cream flavours to choose from and two frozen yoghurts — a lengthy decision. Vuyo opted for a blob of every flavour while Gia monitored the door. Her other eye admired the sauces and tubs of sprinkles available. She twirled mixed-berry frozen yoghurt into the largest cup on offer.

A boy from the birthday gang lit a sparkler and ran around the shop. A *liiiiittle* strange for a kid their age, Gia suspected, while depositing chopped nuts and caramel sauce onto her yoghurt.

'What happened to your foot?' the boy with the sparkler called as he passed her by in his hipster trousers, bright red shirt and back-to-front sailor's cap.

'She broke it!' Vuyo hollered back.

'Duh!' the sparkler-boy gibed.

Vuyo spooned a heaped pile of jellybeans onto his ice cream and swamped them with chocolate sauce. He brought out his phone and snapped a photo of their ice creams, in case Tammy asked. They posed for a selfie — more evidence — and put their cups on the scale at the counter while scanning the food menu. They ordered the largest plate of chips on the menu and some chicken nuggets to share. Gia paid with the money her dad had given her and selected a booth close to the fire-escape. She dug in. It was divine, but she was forced to take a break because of brain-freeze. As a distraction, she pulled their printouts from beneath her blouse and scanned through them. A few pages in, something caught her eye.

'Have you heard of the concept of Finders Keepers?'

'Of course.' Vuyo clicked his tongue, licked his lips. 'Everyone has.'

'Explain.'

'You find something... you keep it.' Vuyo never tried to hide his sarcasm.

'Why don't you give it back?'

'You don't know who to give it to.'

'And if you did?'

'What's this about?'

'Listen to this. It's dated the twelfth of June nineteen-seventy-nine and it's titled, *Finders Keepers — Verdict!*' She began reading. *'It is something of a modern-day fairytale. Once upon a time, on a clear springtide night, a Cape Town sailor discovered a shipwreck. Instead of handing the vessel over to authorities, he claimed Finders Keepers and went into hiding. Finders Keepers is an age-old maritime practice that allows the discoverer of a shipwreck the right to assert ownership to the vessel, including its contents.'*

'I didn't know you could do that.' Vuyo gulped down a jellybean.

'The original insurers of the vessel challenged the sailor's claim in the High Court of South Africa. They argued that they'd paid monies to the owner after the ill-fated journey, and therefore they owned the wreck.

Speculation is rife that the ship in question once belonged to the Earl of Canteridge — The Countess of Stafford's only son. And indeed, unconfirmed reports reveal that the Earl's vessel failed to reach its destination. He was subsequently declared lost-at-sea in August 1962.

Judge Eric Davis ruled that insurers were in that line of work, they received insurance premiums for their efforts and in return, the owner received the insurance payout. Furthermore, because no active search for the vessel was underway, the sailor's claim could stand.'

'He won? No way!' Vuyo stretched his eyes. 'The sailor must be who Oupie bought the guns from.'

'Exactly.' Gia smirked.

Vuyo grabbed some printouts and ran through them while he munched on more jelly beans. 'Here's another one. It's the fifteenth of June nineteen-seventy-nine.'

'The controversial sailor whose legendary claim to a shipwreck, presumably located in False Bay just off the coast of

South Africa, was allegedly rushed to hospital last night under heavy police guard. He was pronounced Dead-on-Arrival.'

'No.' Gia covered her mouth with the back of her hand. 'That's awful.'

'The unnamed sailor was forced out of hiding to attend the verdict of his Finders Keepers challenge — most likely related to a ship that once belonged to the Earl of Canteridge. The notorious sailor is rumoured to have been attacked on his trawler shortly after the judge ruled in his favour.

He died without revealing the location of his find.' Vuyo shot Gia an enquiring glance.

She knew what he was thinking. Where did Oupie get the guns if the sailor never revealed the whereabouts of the Earl's ship?

Vuyo carried on reading. *'In an effort to protect the identity of the sailor's family, Judge Eric Davis, who was himself accosted in his chambers late yesterday evening, ordered that all court records pertaining to the recent Finders Keepers trial, as well as access to any documents referencing the vessel in question, be sealed with immediate effect.'*

Gia dragged the article closer. She bent over squinting at the photograph above it, and gave a strangled gasp before she sat back, clapping both of her hands over her mouth.

'What?' Vuyo frowned.

'Look.'

Vuyo inspected the enhanced but blurry image of a man exiting the courtroom. His clothes were baggy, and he shielded his face by turning it away from photographers. A deep scar slanted across his cheek, and it was blatantly obvious that he didn't have a left ear. 'It looks like the photograph of...' Vuyo looked up. His eyes narrowed. 'Pop?'

'It *is* Pop!' Gia chewed a thumbnail.

Vuyo confiscated her hand, lowering it.

'Ooooh, boyfriend and girlfriend,' the sparkler-boy whined from across the parlour.

Vuyo jumped up, threw one of Gia's nuts at him, then snapped a picture as a way of retaliation. Gia sensed her cheeks flush, so she looked down. Had anyone actually ever died of embarrassment?

The boy invited himself over. 'What school do you guys go to?' He asked plonking himself in their booth. He had short, dark curls, eyes the colour of midnight and a broad-toothed grin that smacked of knee-deep mischief.

'We're homeschooled,' Vuyo replied.

'Ah, shame. That's rotten luck.' And then, 'So what did happen to your foot?'

'Car accident,' Gia said.

'Did it roll?'

'Uh-huh.'

'How many times?'

'I don't know, three, four.'

'Did you think you were a goner?' He stared at her with a glint of approval, but one of his friends dumping an upside-down ice cream cup on his head, crowning him as King of the Parlour interrupted him. The boy rushed off to defend his honour.

'Are you thinking what I'm thinking?' Gia checked with Vuyo, watching a gum-snapping waitress deliver their nuggets and chips.

'That it's the *Velox* that sank? It's the ship Pop found, it's where Oupie got the guns from and probably the scroll. That ship is what this complete mess is about.' Vuyo shovelled a fork full of chips into his mouth and chewed with intensity.

Gia twisted her mouth to the side. 'Actually, I was thinking this article proves that Oupie's stuck in the scroll.'

Vuyo's eyes stretched. 'How do you figure?' He sprinkled salt onto their chips and doused them with vinegar.

'Because after what happened to Pop, he'd know that hiding wouldn't solve anything. And he wouldn't rush off if he knew people were after us because of this. No way.' Gia shook her head. 'All these years Oupie spent telling your mom that his guns are worthless. He wasn't lying. They were worthless — to him! He knew if he sold them that this could happen because they're traceable.'

'So it's my mom's fault?'

'No, of course not. How would she have known?'

'But when she presented Worldwide Valuations Incorporated with that gun, it was as if she'd announced to every antique dealer on the planet that the *Velox* hadn't only been found, but also salvaged.'

They bobbed thoughtful heads, and Gia felt wise for finally knowing why her life had been thrown into the washer.

'What's your name?' The sparkler-boy had returned.

Gia put her elbows over their newspaper articles, dragging them surreptitiously towards herself.

'I'm Vuyo, and this is Gia.'

'I'm Tito. How old are you guys?'

'Twelve,' Vuyo murmured.

'It's Vuyo's birthday today,' Gia yapped and Vuyo smiled a shy smile.

'Really? I'll be twelve in two weeks!'

'That's cool,' Vuyo grinned.

'Wanna come?'

'Pardon?' Vuyo's face froze.

'Wanna come to my party? My mom said I can invite as many kids as I want. She says the best part of high school is making new friends and I guess you won't have many opportunities if you're homeschooled,' Tito informed them, chest puffed out.

'Maybe I will,' Vuyo threatened with a lopsided grin. He tucked a rogue hair behind his ear before shovelling another bunch of chips into his mouth.

'We aren't allowed to have long hair at the high school I go to. You'd get in so much trouble.'

'Ah. So there *are* perks to being homeschooled?' Vuyo chirped.

'See you in two weeks then. And bring your girlfriend,' Tito ordered, with a whiff of superiority. He went off with an important swagger and as if Vuyo wouldn't dream of declining his invitation.

'Look at you, making friends wherever you go. Aren't you the lucky skull,' Gia teased.

Vuyo glanced around the room with a gaze that was half-way suspicious. 'Gia, I think Detective Steel knows that Oupie's guns came off the *Velox, which mean*s he probably knows about the

Finders Keepers Trial, and that's why he gave us better guards. But because the judge sealed the records, he hasn't yet figured out that the sailor who claimed the ship is related to you and Oupie. The minute someone — anyone — realises that you are. They could end up thinking you know where the treasure is.'

Gia shrivelled her nose up, gobsmacked. 'Nobody said anything about treasure.'

'Nobody had to. Duh!' Vuyo stretched his eyes. 'Can you think of another reason Pop would claim a shipwreck?'

'The scroll.' Gia battered her eyes.

Vuyo clicked his tongue. 'Pop wouldn't have endangered the lives of his family for something that he didn't know for a fact was valuable. No way! And anyway, it's not about what the *Velox* carried, it's about what people *think* it carried. That's why everyone wants to know where Oupie got the guns from.' Vuyo tapped his index finger repeatedly on the table. 'The *Velox* is what Hunter Scott and that other fellow are looking for. The *Velox* is the reason Deon Sanderson was on our bridge. What their actions prove, Gia, is that people believe — rightly or wrongly — that those guns aren't the only things that went down on that ship.'

Gia folded her arms, leaned back and stared over Vuyo's head into that faraway space, thinking it through. 'And we know where her ultimate resting place is. *"What some would hide, this scroll would let you see."'* She quoted the passage from the book she'd seen in the library and told him about the rest of it.

Vuyo dropped his jaw in an exaggerated gape, mischievous eyes shining like jewels. 'The plateau. That's why there's a gate, it's the reason for the boulders, the riddle and the key. *And* the reason we saw the *Velox* in the scroll's vision — because it had to have been her — is that the scroll remembers what happened in a place. And we already know that ship's resting place is a secret because the riddle said as much. *Those who know thereof, do not speak,*' Vuyo breathed.

'Let's look for her. But this time, keep your eyes peeled for Oupie while we're inside those visions. He's got to be in one of them, just like your cap,' Gia whispered.

'You're jumping to conclusions. What about Bongi's warning? And the fact that some people call this thing the Banishing scroll,' Vuyo croaked.

'All I know is that if using the scroll is how Oupie got himself trapped inside it, then using the scroll is the only way to get him back out. How else are we going to do it? We don't have any other magic, and we owe him that much. The plateau seems the logical place to look because its where the secret starts.'

Vuyo gave her a hard stare through narrow eyes. 'I've been thinking about something too. We've been assuming that Oupie knew everything we know just because of those guns. But what if Pop removed them from the *Velox* before the outcome of the trial and before they attacked him? What if Oupie was searching for answers too?'

'And got himself trapped in the process?'

'It it's true, it means we can't ignore Bongi's warning, Gia.'

Gia stroked her chin, considering. 'Let's test what we know before we take any more risks. If the scroll reveals secrets, which is what we think it does, there's a secret it's already shown us which we haven't followed up on.'

'The dungeon,' Vuyo breathed, flicking his eyebrows.

'And we're going to find it... tonight.'

Chapter 18:

Opportunity for answers

Gia steered clear of her dad, not to mention the piano.

After dinner, they feasted on Tammy's double-decker chocolate cake, sucked the air from helium balloons and played Repeat-after-me. It wasn't long before everybody, including Elias, began acting as if they spoke Giggle, trying but failing to choke out stories between reams of laughter. It did nothing to calm Gia's nerves. She could hardly believe that they still hadn't mentioned Mister Coat or Hunter Scott to their parents or that they'd got away with things and now, well, they'd begun plotting again. The mystery surrounding Oupie's disappearance had… grown. But they were close. She was sure.

At ten, Gia deviously piled mattresses into the lounge and began watching action movies because a boy's birthday wasn't complete unless he'd watched someone blow stuff up.

Vuyo pretended to fall asleep and Gia turned off the lights but left the TV droning as loudly as she dared. A scenario designed to swallow the suspicious sounds they'd be trying not to make. They launched their investigation while a blustering wind howled and thunder growled. Occasionally it shook the corners of the house as if it fancied ripping it from its foundation.

Gia waited for the grandfather clock to chime midnight. Dressed in her panda pyjamas, she woke Jinja and invited her along. What choice did they have? It was that or risk her whining — maybe yodelling — from her bedroom. Nina, on the other hand, seemed quite content having the bed all to herself.

Gia left her moonboot beside her bed and tiptoed in a manner that would have made Catwoman proud. She stole a cautious look down the passage. Guilt bubbled in her throat while her heartbeat pounded in her ears. No doubt it disapproved of this slippery slope to delinquent hood she was skidding along.

They ducked down, crawling along the cool floor, pausing each time moonlight peeped through clouds. Gia tilted her head, listened. Thunder clapped, somewhere something clack-clacked. There was a snort from the porch. A guard struck a match. Dread twitched Gia's stomach. It wouldn't pay to be mistaken for thieves. And even if they survived that, Tammy would kill them.

Jinja's toenails scratched the floor. Vuyo stiffened and his breathing came a little faster.

Finally, they closed the door to the study and Gia heaved a sigh, allowing her shoulders to slacken while she ran her bare feet along the fluffy carpet. Disappointingly, the scent of Oupie's tobacco had diminished.

Vuyo inched towards the window and twisted the mechanism to close the blinds, minuscule movements at a time. He walked into the couch. Gia heard him grunt, 'Ouch!' Something clicked. A muted glow from Oupie's stained-glass Tiffany lamp flicked on.

They locked eyes and Gia saw the same worry reflected on Vuyo's face.

They waited. Nobody came.

Vuyo began checking behind furniture. He lay on the floor and peered under cupboards and moved ornaments, searching for clues. Gia glimpsed behind paintings and raided Oupie's display case. She turned things upside-down, scrutinising them for top-secret buttons, even coasted a hand under the cushions of Oupie's couch, mimicking the actions of the police officer who'd searched her bedroom.

'There's nothing here,' Vuyo griped.

Gia ignored him. She moved Oupie's desk chair and went onto her knees, unpacking the desk's drawers. Putting the binoculars, telescope and Oupie's rusty pocket-watch on top of the desk, she slid the drawers from their chambers and packed them oh-so-carefully onto the ground, determined not to make a sound. 'Does your cellphone have a torch?'

Vuyo nodded. He knelt beside her and shone a light into the gaps the drawers normally filled. 'There aren't any secret buttons in here, Gia. The police would have found them if there were, anyway.'

A jolt of lightning flashed for a chilling second, shedding light on the little red button beneath Oupie's desk.

Gia's heart pulsed almost electrically and skipped a few beats. She sat straighter, and an idea fizzed in her brain. 'Vuyo, that's it! What if the button isn't a secret? The police wouldn't have thought twice about it then. They'd assume it implied something obvious. Same as we did.' Gia pointed at the red button. 'What if the entrance to the dungeon was hidden in plain sight?'

'Nah-uh.' Vuyo looked sceptical. 'Not if it's hiding treasure, no way. Too simple.'

Gia skirted forward.

'Don't!' Vuyo tussled to drag her back.

Too late.

She jabbed the button with her index finger.

Click! Clack! Snap!

Gia sensed a subtle tremor and her breath hitched in anticipation.

It stopped.

'Told you!' Vuyo jeered but came close to having a seizure when the grandfather clock ding-donged one o'clock.

Gia giggled like a sprite at Vuyo's fright. 'Something happened. Don't pretend you didn't feel it too!'

'It must be a double lock, then. And the second one won't be a button, that would be too easy.'

'What about something that could link to a code?' Gia jerked her chin towards the grandfather clock. 'Something that could act as a number pad?'

'I suppose. The clock's too noisy, though. If you move the hour-hand past the twelve it chimes, every time.'

Fair point, Gia decided and racked her brain for another sensible place to look while reinserting the desk's drawers and putting the binoculars, telescope and pocket-watch back where she'd found them. She was about to close the drawer, but her thoughts boomeranged. 'Wait, a minute.' Gia raised the pocket-watch. 'What about this? Why would Oupie hang onto a rusty watch?'

They bumped their heads together and Vuyo bobbed his head. 'It's a calendar watch.'

'Meaning?'

'It shows not only the time but also the date in the middle circle. Day, month, year.'

'Try Oupie's birthday!' Gia ordered and her neck hairs pricked.

Vuyo moved the dials.

The watch kept ticking.

'Try Oumie's.'

Tick-tock, tick-tock.

They ran through everyone's birthdays. None worked.

'How about the numbers of those hives that Oupie left to your dad?' Gia suggested.

Vuyo moved the dial to 4-8-20.

There was a tremor beneath her feet. A creak. *What on earth?*

Jinja bolted onto the couch. There was another sound of splitting wood and the patch of carpet on which the desk chair normally stood trembled and shook. A square, no bigger than a trapdoor, popped up a smidgen and a rush of stale air invaded the room as the carpet swivelled effortlessly sideways.

At their feet, a staircase dug its way into a dark cement pit that could be a dungeon, a prison, maybe a secret tunnel. Gia just hoped it wasn't a grave.

'Are you sure you want to go in there?' Vuyo croaked.

'No.'

'Wanna leave it?'

'Nah.' And because she knew her mind would soon begin conjuring ghosts, vampires and many nasty creatures, Gia slurped a breath. She pressed her lips together and descended into something that felt like a dark and mouldy fridge. Could this be where Oupie was hiding? Why would he do that? Perhaps it was the place she'd seen Elias searching for in Oupie's bedroom? She stopped, straining her ear to the gap, extra vigilant. 'I don't hear any noises.'

'I should hope not,' Vuyo squeezed his nose closed, flicked on his cellphone's torch and took the lead, ignoring the little cobweb inventors who scrambled for corners.

As they stepped from the last rung onto a red-brick floor, muffled lamps snapped to life along the top edges of the walls. They shed light on a room that was dreary as sand. And small. Three metres squared, give-or-take. Gia looked around, expecting a labyrinth of tunnels at the very least. Maybe even something that connected to the plateau.

'A wine cellar?' Gia gaped at the wall of corks that looked ready to shoot if anyone dared them to.

'Look on that side.' Vuyo pointed at the wall behind the stairs.

A shelved case stretched from the roof to floor with row upon row of antique toy cars still dressed in original packaging. They were individually protected from dust by glass casings and organised according to dates ranging from 1908 to 1925.

'I don't understand. Why would Oupie have a secret dungeon filled with something everyone knows he buys and sells?' Vuyo puzzled, looking crestfallen by the lack of treasure.

Gia bit hard on her lip. This day was getting long, but her gut claimed that there was more to this place than what met the eye. There had to be a reason for Oupie to have kept this dungeon a secret. Elias once told her that if she was searching for something, she should move your eyes anti-clockwise. Gia turned slow as a sloth, scanning every brick until she spotted an oddball. It wasn't significant, just a brick that it stood slightly proud at the base of the steps.

She stepped on it and lamps flickered spookily.

'There! That brick's also raised.' Vuyo pointed at a spot on the floor close to the toy cabinet. He stamped on it.

Nothing.

'Try them together.' Gia said. 'On three! One, two, three!'

The sound of stone sliding on stone.

A brick at waist height centred between them dropped from the wall.

Crash!

A mechanical shelf-like mechanism slid eerily from the hole the falling brick had created. On it was a book, dull, weathered, but on display like a coffin in a church and bound in leather the colour of muddied earth and closed with copper clasps.

Not what Gia had hoped for but better than nothing.

An opportunity for answers, perhaps?

Chapter 19:

The twelfth passenger

A mad scramble and a chattering of excitement erupted as they began juggling ideas. They returned the wristwatch to Oupie's desk drawer after moving the dials back to today's date. Making sure they covered their tracks, they crawled back along the icy wooden floor.

'Hurry! Let me see!' Vuyo settled on Gia's couch with the yellow giraffes still sprinting across its fabric. She threw a robe over her shoulders and pulled her feet up, crossing her legs, enjoying the feel of being able to take her moonboot off for short periods and do normal things without the weight of a clumsy lead balloon on her foot.

Vuyo nicked the journal while she wasn't looking. They jostled for control and Vuyo won by elbowing her in the ribs. He smirked as he pulled the clasp open.

The pages were tacky. Their edges damp, yellowing but jam-packed with tall, untidy strokes that bent backwards.

'This isn't Oupie's handwriting,' Gia whispered.

'Whose is it, then?' Vuyo chimed.

Gia shrugged.

The book was structured in the manner of a diary. The first page had a simple heading: *Velox.* From there it jumped straight into the juice of what they were after, subtly revealing the author's identity.

Without providing coordinates, the writer described his find.

1977

February 3rd

Whatever her story, the vessel met a violent death.

I suspect the skipper mistook False Bay for Table Bay. It's how the name originated, after all. And it's the only thing that makes sense. By the look of her, there's no doubt she was travelling at full speed with trailing winds when she incurred the mountain's wrath.

'This is Pop's journal,' Gia hissed.

'It's got to be,' Vuyo agreed.

The mountain has collapsed around her.

She's wedged between crags. A carcass incarcerated in a tomb of her own making. The gaps above her have closed over by foliage.

I only found her because I came into the cave through the water. And because I've spent weeks investigating air-pockets that intrigued me. It's immodest to say, but... I can hold my breath for far longer than the average man.

Deep inside the mountain, the entrance was. Dark.

By the grace of God, I left markings. If I hadn't, I would never have found my way out, and it's plain to see that no one would have found me.

Vuyo gasped and turned the page.

February 4th

She used to be a grand Galleon — a three-mast sailing ship.

What's left of her keel has rocks poking through like thorns into a shoe. Rot has gnawed away most of her bow. Her foremast and mainmast are cracked - snapped clean off - and the superstructure of her main deck has crumbled.

She was lost a while ago, I'd say.

Decade, maybe more.

They got a glimpse of the ship. Pop had drawn pencil sketches.

'Gosh, there wasn't much left of her, was there?' said Vuyo.

'Look here.' Gia tapped a drawing.

'That's Oupie's desk, and that's his telescope!'

'And that's the gate from the cave. It came off the ship!' Vuyo tapped another sketch.

February 6th

I've discovered a cargo of crates deep in the cave — Toy cars — Antiques.

They're still in boxes.

Gia shared a glance with Vuyo. 'I guess that means you've already found your treasure.'

February 7th

The crates don't have water damage.

It can only mean one thing.

Survivors.

Vuyo sucked in his breath and Gia put her hands over her mouth. It took a while for them to pluck up the guts to turn the page.

They were trapped by the mountain.

It's impossible to say for how long.

They never made it.

'No,' Gia breathed.

Without knowing about those air-pockets and exactly which route to take, escape was never on the cards. It's unlikely the foliage existed back then. If it did, they might have had a go at climbing. Difficult to say. I don't know for sure if the plant would hold the weight of a man.

They died long, lingering deaths.

Starvation... dehydration, probably.

'That's awful,' Gia breathed, sadness swallowing her up.

Eleven corpses.

Adults. All male.

February 9th

Can't bring myself to disturb their remains.

Doesn't seem right.

February 10th

Two of the crates have secret compartments.

And so does the captain's desk.

'That's the treasure I'm talking about!' Vuyo said, and his eyes sparkled with wicked pleasure.

February 11th

I've put my reservations aside. These folks deserve proper burials.

I can't conceivably bring them back through the water, though.

I'll just have to find another way in.

February 12th

Found the manifest — twelve passengers.

Names are illegible. The document is crumbly.

It was most likely submerged for some time.

The missing passenger might have gone for help... or died while the vessel was still at sea. In which case, he would have been thrown overboard.

That's my guess.

I should be able to trace the ship.

Might try.

Pop explained how he had made a trapdoor by disassembling a crate before he sealed the cavern.

April 5th

She belonged to the Earl of Canteridge.

He was aboard the Velox.

The poor soul died without heirs, which isn't to say he had no children, it simply means he had no sons.

'What? A girl's an heir too! That's not fair!' Gia prattled her five cent worth.

May 1st

I've decided to claim her. The cargo's worth a pretty penny.

If not now, soon enough.

'He could be referring to the toys,' Gia murmured. 'Oupie once told me how he sold one of those little cars for the price of a real one.'

We need the money. The bank has called twice.

They suggest I sell part of the land and pay what I owe, but Samuel wants to build a factory. The cargo will cover that. Easily.

I've instructed my attorney to launch the claim anonymously if he can.

Seems sensible to err on the side of caution.

Who would guess the Velox lies beneath MY mountain?

They'd assume I found her at sea.

Of course they would.

Besides, if the Earl doesn't have any heirs, she doesn't belong to anybody.

Not anymore.

The next inserts were newspaper clippings and long-worded lawyers letters related to the long, blah-blah, drawn-out legal proceedings of Pop's unprecedented Finders Keepers trial during which, Gia couldn't help notice, he was called many cruel things. The next comment Pop wrote was midway through the journal.

1978

October

Attacked. Left for dead. Lost my ear.

They didn't leave my face very pretty either.

The family's in danger. I suspect.

Vuyo shot Gia a worried glance.

She turned the page and found a folded blue document, opened it, and stiffened.

1978

December

Petition for Name Change.

Samuel Gallagher Lynch to Samuel George Morgan.

Gia blinked and blinked, then paged anxiously. Just how much danger had the family been in? She found a copy of a signed Deed of Transfer granting ownership of Polymead Grove to Samuel George Morgan.

Three pages on, she discovered a lah-di-dah envelope with gold trimmings. She pulled out a note. 'It's just a lawyer's letter.'

'Read it! It's different from the others. It could be about the verdict!' Vuyo commanded.

'Dear Mister Lynch

Allow me to introduce myself. I am the representative of Annamay Gracelyn Stafford, 2nd Countess of Stafford, countess suo jure. It saddens me-'

'That's the Earl's mother,' Vuyo knitted his brow. 'But what does *suo jure* mean? Do you know?'

Gia fetched her laptop. Into the Google search engine, she typed: SUO JURE. 'It's a Latin phrase that means *in her own right.*'

'Ah, clear as mud, then.' Vuyo sounded frustrated.

Gia tapped away at the keyboard, searching for COUNTESS OF STAFFORD. 'It says here that the Countess married the Earl of Canteridge. They had a son who inherited his father's peerage because he was a male of body. But because their son didn't have male heirs, the Canteridge peerage is extinct until the Queen gives it to someone else. Apparently, she can do that. But the Countess, Lady Stafford, was never dependant on her husband for a title. She inherited a peerage from her paternal father. It's Scottish, the most ancient in Britain, dating from the twelve hundreds and it can be *dissolved upon heirs general.*' Gia used her index fingers to put the phrase into quotation marks. 'According to this, that means Lady Stafford's title can pass to a male or female heir. And she has a niece, so the peerage will go to her.' Gia glanced up. 'Vuyo, Lady Stafford's still alive.'

'No way.'

'Yes, way. She's ninety-one.' Gia switched back to the solicitor's letter and continued from where she'd left off. '*It saddens me that our first communication should occur under circumstances such as these.*

Firstly, rest assured that the Countess has no desire to assert proprietorship of the Velox.'

'That means she didn't want to claim ownership of the ship,' Vuyo prattled.

'*The vessel begot nothing but anguish, despair and immense grief. Her requests are personal and, we believe, reasonable.*

There is one earthly item she wishes for you to revert — their family heirloom — a writing desk. Lady Stafford hopes that it was salvageable. Most likely positioned in one of the sleeping chambers. As I'm sure you're able to discern, the item is of negligible value.'

'She wanted the scroll!' Vuyo sang. 'If you ask me, the scroll is the heirloom and Lady Stafford knew about that secret compartment in the desk, she just couldn't say so directly.'

Gia bobbed. '*Furthermore, at our expense, naturally, Lady Stafford requests the repatriation to Scotland of the Earl's remains and those of his...*' Gia's throat went dry.

'What?' Vuyo's eyes stretched. 'Gia!' He snatched the letter and read for himself. '*Lady Stafford requests the repatriation to Scotland of the Earl's remains and those of his... three-year-old daughter.'* Vuyo's hand went to his mouth. *'She wishes for her loved ones to join their ancestors in the family burial ground, in keeping with their family tradition.'*

'Look what Pop wrote at the bottom of the letter.' Gia pointed, her eyes brimming with unexpected tears.

Vuyo's gaze flitted to the edge of the letter where Pop's sprawling bent-over-backwards writing lingered. *'Twelfth passenger? Even I couldn't mistake the remains of a female toddler for that of a male corpse. One thing I'm certain of — the Earl's daughter is not in the cave.'* Vuyo rubbed his index fingers against his temple. 'Maybe she died at sea and the Earl threw her overboard,' he suggested in a voice that had become low and thick.

Gia balled herself up. 'I don't see why he'd do that if they had a family burial ground.'

Vuyo's eyes smouldered while he scanned the rest of the lawyer's letter. 'There's one more request. Listen. *Lastly, the Countess would be obliged if you allowed her to visit the shipwreck so she can pay her respects to the dead in the hope that it will bring her closure. Thanking you kindly.'*

It was as if someone had struck a match and burned away the fog in her head. 'This is it! This is why people are after us. We've had the angle wrong. What if Lady Stafford wanted the desk because she wanted the scroll? If we're right, and she used it at the site of the shipwreck, it would show her what happened on the *Velox.* Maybe she even wanted to confirm for herself that the Earl and his daughter were dead. Because until someone knows for sure, it's a secret, isn't it?'

Vuyo grabbed her idea and joined a few more dots. 'But someone didn't want her to know, so they came after Pop. And it must have been someone close to her if they knew about the scroll. Those same people could be involved with what happened on our bridge.' He twisted his mouth to the side and dropped his voice. 'Because it seems to me that someone out there *still* doesn't want Lady Stafford to get her hands on that thing.'

'And they definitely wouldn't want her thinking that her granddaughter might have survived.' Gia crinkled her nose while the hairs on her neck scoffed at the scandal. 'So what *we've* got to do is get the answer for Lady Stafford and then get it to her.'

'We can't go around using the scroll willy-nilly,' Vuyo grunted. 'Bongi was right about what it shows, Gia. So was the book you read in the library. So they're probably right about the risk, too. And let's not forget, the last time we opened that thing on the plateau, it almost killed you. If we go there searching for a ship, there's a good chance we'll end up in the water again.'

'Then we'll take life-jackets.'

'Get a grip, Gia.' Vuyo's jaw set. 'I know it sounds selfish but… what happened on the *Velox* is irrelevant. We can only risk using the scroll for things that help *us*.'

'I am gripped.' Gia clutched Vuyo by the chest and rocked him back and forth. 'It will help us. Don't you see? This is about more than finding Oupie now, it's about protecting our families. We can do that by telling Lady Stafford what she needs to know. She can even have the scroll if she wants it, but only after we've found Oupie. The minute she gets the information she wants, these people lose their power over us and her and the threat to everyone at Polymead Grove goes away.'

'I didn't think of that.' Vuyo ran his tongue along his lips as if deliberating. 'I suppose that we were planning to re-look at the vision on the plateau,' he whispered.

'Exactly.'

'But if someone found the riddle, they could also be there.'

'We'll be careful. Careful is my middle name. All we've got to do is make sure that we stay aboard long enough to search for Oupie and get a glimpse of the passengers. If the Earl's daughter was there, she might have survived.'

Chapter 20:

A sense of blood

The thing about cows was, they needed routine. Anyone working with them had a rigid routine. Gia conspired with Vuyo to use their dad's routine against them.

Their fathers were up at the crack of dawn.

So were they.

Their fathers strolled out the door before five.

So did they.

Elias greeted the guards and Gia's dad handed out mugs of steaming coffee, stopping for an idle chinwag, she snuck out of the back door dressed like a cheerful swamp troll: life-jacket under a red raincoat, yellow scarf, orange cap and pink gumboots.

'You should have worn black!' Vuyo moaned.

'I don't wear black. It isn't a colour,' Gia hissed.

The wind whipped back and forth. Raindrops flew sideways and stung like needles in their faces. Every crack in the land transformed into a canal. They slipped and slid across the yard in squelching mud, alert as hunting dogs until they rolled over the four-foot wall and used it as a shield to spy on the house. They spied on its twinkling lights for a minute.

'Clear!' Vuyo egged Gia on.

She stashed one of her crutches and sacrificed speed for stealth by shunning the road, sneaking from bush to bush and acting like a pretty good outlaw, she thought. But her foot grew tired, so Vuyo carried her on his back and she carried Jinja plus her spare crutch across the backpack on hers. They ordered Jinja to bark if she caught a whiff of anything or anyone and she jumped straight to it, growling at the thunder.

Gia kept an insistent grip around Vuyo's neck and thanked her lucky stars he was cat-footed because they might as well have been water-skiing the way he leapt and bounced down the hill.

The river was a nightmare of swirling black. Its belly bulged, threatening to burst, branches coiled like whips, and the thwack of thunder drew ever nearer. Gia soon began doubting their puffed-up wisdom.

They stopped to wring their scarves, breathing in freezing air tinted with the glorious pong of salt and freshly watered swamp. Wind nibbled at their coats. The rain became bearable too. The thunder, not so much. She remembered her mom saying that it was the sound of clouds bumping together because they enjoyed cuddling too. Nothing at all to worry about.

Gia eyed the waterfall. 'It's a death trap.'

Vuyo glanced at the neon-green symbols on his watch. 'We need to hurry. If we don't get behind that waterfall before it's light, we'll be found, dragged back to the house and convicted before we have time to investigate.' He took her by the elbow. 'It's now or never, Gia. Are you sure that you want to carry on?'

Gia breathed a hefty gulp of air, took her time with the exhale, and stepped onto the first rock. Water rushed around her moonboot, darting devilishly in unpredictable directions with a force that surprised and unnerved her. Every instinct in her body screamed at her to flee. She gritted her teeth and focused on an image of Oupie. She had to save him, no matter what. Somehow, she had to stop these people from coming after them.

Gia took another step and another until they'd climbed behind the waterfall. By the time the door rotated, she seemed to have lost the ability to warm herself, and the river had turned the cave's floor into a muck-sucking mess.

The plateau, on the other hand, was glorious at dawn. Spanking rain had dwindled into a drip and plop. The air smelled fresh and citrus-like despite the brutal wind rustling through shrubs as if playing an angry melody. Table Mountain loitered beneath a patchy sky that had cleared in the way-off distance. Suspicious insects watched them. Something did. Gia thought she detected eyes on her.

Vuyo took the rucksack. He clenched his hands doggedly around the straps and stomped a beeline towards the shed, man-on-a-mission to get the ball rolling.

Gia hobbled after him, blowing into her hands.

Jinja took refuge beneath its last bits of the roof, curling up on the coiled rope as if it were a bed.

'Let me hold the scroll, Gia, in case we end up in the water again. You focus on holding your breath and I'll make sure I end the vision if it gets too dangerous.'

Gia nodded and without further discussion, Vuyo dropped their rucksack, leaned her crutch against the hut and pulled the scroll from its tube. He stepped into the clearing. 'On three. Ready? One. Two. Three.'

The rain stopped, the wind dropped, a blinding flash of sunlight forced Gia's eyes into slits and a rhythmic creaking sound came from the hut. She spun and felt as if someone had given her a whack.

On the hut's porch, staring across False Bay, Elias rode a rocking chair the way a cowboy rode a horse. Except that he couldn't be much older than they were now. Similar to Vuyo, but different in the manner he carried himself. Even at a young age, Elias had the posture of a plank.

Moving only her eyes, Gia checked Vuyo for his reaction, unsure how it would play out because, truth was, she couldn't help but feel a bit annoyed. The vision confirmed that Elias had known about the plateau all along. Which implied that he also knew about the Finders Keepers trial. And if Oupie was stuck in the scroll, he must have given her the key.

Vuyo made a sound between a surly snort and an I-don't-believe-it cackle. He closed the scroll. '*Those who know thereof do not speak.* And we both know that my dad doesn't waffle at the best of times,' he whispered with a sour snort. But before Gia could respond, he reopened the scroll.

Gia blinked around.

The sun had bid farewell. Silver flecks of light rippled across the sea and the thud of heavy footsteps approached them.

Elias burst from behind the curtain of reeds, sprinting full chisel. He wore a tousled shirt, his face was sweaty and disgruntled, and his eyes appeared troubled. 'Samuel!' he bellowed. 'Are you here?'

Vuyo grabbed Gia by the hand and hauled her behind the hut. She crumpled onto her knees and peered round the planks.

'Samuel!' Elias slowed. He halted in the centre of the plateau, raking a slow glance around. Walking towards the furthermost cliff, he crouched onto his haunches. With two fingers and an inquisitorial scowl, he retrieved something from the ground, holding it at an arm's length.

The scroll.

Gia's mouth went dry. She knew which vision she was seeing — the day Oupie had disappeared.

Cautious as a cat, Elias unrolled the scroll.

What would he see? What if a vision within a vision was dangerous? Maybe that's how Oupie got himself trapped?

Nothing happened.

Elias continued gazing at the parchment. He turned it over, blew across the white, chalky flakes and watched almost absent mindedly as they wafted over the cliff. He slipped the scroll into its tube, buried it in his pocket and staggered back across the plateau. His legs seemed heavy and Gia could have sworn he was crying.

'I don't understand. Why didn't the scroll show my dad anything?' Vuyo closed the scroll, frowning at it. 'And how come it isn't showing me the *Velox?*'

'Of course. It's said to have a sense of place, which is triggered by its sense of blood.' Gia whispered as the truth of the words washed over her. 'I didn't understand what it meant before.'

Vuyo's eyes narrowed and his forehead crumped. 'So… you think the scroll isn't showing me the *Velox* — it can't — because I'm not related to Oupie or Pop by blood?'

'Wouldn't that explain why it showed us your dad's secrets — because you're related to him? And it never showed *him* anything because his relatives have never been on the plateau? So there aren't any secrets in his bloodline. Not here,' Gia whispered.

'That makes sense, but… then I'm confused about why we saw the *Velox* crash. Pop wasn't on it, he didn't see it happen so…?' Vuyo crinkled his nose.

'You're right. It's weird.' Gia nibbled her lip.

'Let's worry about figuring the visions out later.' Vuyo flipped over his wrist, handing Gia the scroll. 'Right now, we need to hurry up and get back so that my mom can kill us.'

Gia chuckled unexpectedly. 'Ready?'

'You bet.' Vuyo took her hand and slid his fingers between hers.

Gia unrolled the scroll. She held it open with her thumb and index finger, preparing to brace.

Things differed from the get-go.

The sun was rising. The roar of the sea, absolute and fog the colour of cement haunted the horizon, bringing with it that crisp, salty odour. Boulders shielding them from the cliff face ceased to exist. The plateau sloped, became jagged, and they found themselves on a slice of ground that pitched towards the sea. It was so steep that Vuyo pulled them into a crouch to ensure they didn't lose their footing.

'I don't see anything!' Gia shouted above the roaring sea.

'There!' Vuyo pointed.

Ahead of them, from a gap in the ground, crawled a fine-boned, white-haired wisp of a girl covered in muck. She stopped to glance downwards.

What on earth? Gia's heart leapt into a gallop and something stirred in her memory. Leaning ever-so-slightly forward, she peered over the precipice in the direction of the girl's gaze. What greeted her was a sight so bizarre it had to be real.

Sandwiched between gaps of rock and almost inside the mountain, way below, eleven men on the deck of a banged-up ship stared up at her with expectation on their faces.

The girl inched closer to the ridge of the cliff. She stood, sprang over a gap, then sank back onto her knees, clambering onto another outcrop of rocks.

She was crying. Not that subtle sob that came from misery, but an awful penetrating wail that spoke of downright terror. The world became sluggish and Gia blinked into the early morning breeze, grappling with the sight while her mind played hide-and-seek with a memory. Something about the girl was… familiar.

'That must be Lady Stafford's granddaughter,' Vuyo said.

Just then the girl glanced up with enormous blue eyes. Her eyelids were puffy and surrounded by glistening rings of red, and Gia's memory threatened to give.

'She looks like…' Vuyo gasped and his eyes ping-ponged between Gia, the girl, Gia and the girl as if watching a tennis match. But before Gia could answer. 'She's too close to the edge!' Vuyo broke into a sprint. He reached the cliff and threw himself forward, landing with his stomach on a rock as a smack of sea sprayed over its crest.

'Vuyo! Don't! She isn't real!' Gia hollered.

The girl looked towards him and in the split-second that her gaze met Vuyo's, she slipped.

'Grab my hand!' Vuyo lunged forward.

'Vuyo!' Gia shrieked.

'Quickly! Grab it!' Vuyo yelled. He slithered over the rock on his belly, focused. A second wave broke, bigger, more powerful. It crashed onto his back.

Gia made a decision that took a split-second to regret. She released the scroll in the same instant that the girl reached for Vuyo's hand.

As their fingers touched, he vanished.

A blinding flash of light burst from the parchment. From inside the light came a high-pitched scream that echoed but didn't break for breath.

Gia's skin prickled with goosebumps and a vile taste spread through her mouth as if her spittle had curdled. Seagulls whirled into the air. Boulders shielding the plateau from the sea snapped back into place.

And before her, shimmery at first, a shadowy old man hunched over a cane.

Chapter 21:

Lady Stafford's granddaughter

'I'm waiting for my granddaughter, have you seen her?' A raspy voice that Gia would have recognised anywhere drawled.

Oupie might have sounded like the voice of innocence. He looked anything but. A purple scar ate into his arm. He was bald as a beet, with a paper-white beard and sparkling diamond earring. His muddied shirt was unbuttoned, displaying his furry chest and bobbling belly. The red sneakers he'd worn on the day of the accident were still on his feet.

Gia trembled, unable to speak. Slow and dreamlike, Oupie moved towards her, his cane making a tok-tok sound. She stepped back.

Oupie swallowed his chapped lips. 'Well? Have you? She's about this big.' He croaked and raised his scarred arm to Gia's head height, delight flickering in his eyes.

Gia's every instinct craved to hug him. But common sense told her to be careful, the chances of Oupie being real were almost zero. Where had Oupie come from — the scroll? Was he a ghost? Part of a more recent vision? She couldn't tear her eyes away. She looked for Vuyo. Had he fallen from the rocks? The idea made Gia's heartbeat quicken.

Squawk-squawk! The seagulls continued squabbling.

It was a chore snubbing the man she'd been longing for. She stood on her toes, trying to ignore her heart slamming against her ribcage and making her feel nauseous. Gia peered gingerly over Oupie's shoulder, torn between the sight of him and the tragedy of the spot where Vuyo had been shouting moments earlier.

'Vuyo?' Gia's eyes prowled the cliff. 'Vuyo!'

Gia couldn't shake the feeling that Vuyo had switched places with Oupie. *Stray too long where you don't belong and the world you're from could be forever gone.* Perhaps because he'd tried to help Grace? Could touching someone in one of the scroll's visions mean that he'd strayed where he didn't belong?

A luke-warm idea popped into her head. A stretch.

Gia scouted the ground for the scroll, found it bobbing in a puddle. From where she stood, she couldn't tell if it was open or closed. Perhaps if she unrolled it and closed it again — a reset — maybe, just maybe, Vuyo would reappear. If Oupie stayed where he was, she'd know he was real. If not, he'd been imaginary to begin with. A chance she'd have to take.

She stepped towards the puddle.

'Don't!' A commanding voice, quick with alarm, barked.

It's odd accent set fire to Gia's already kindling gut. She twisted, her eyes widening at the sight of a raincoat covered figure emerging from the Orange Grove. How had he come through the gate? His presence is what confirmed that Vuyo was missing, but Oupie was as real as real could be.

And so was Hunter Scott.

Gia blinked and blinked, stepping back without a smoggy clue what to make of this twist in her tale. All she knew was that she didn't have time to muck about, not now — they needed to get away from him. How could she do that *and* find Vuyo?

Without warning, Oupie's legs went rubbery. He swayed and Gia lurched forward, straining to hold him. 'Get away from us!' she shouted at Hunter in a squeaky voice, choking back tears, grappling with how fragile Oupie had become.

Hunter scuttled in and kind-heartedly gathered Oupie around his waist. He steadied his burden by carry-walking him towards the nearest rock. 'Are you alright… Samuel?' he asked and his brow creased.

'I'm sorry but… who are you?' Oupie rasped.

'I saw a ship a-sailing, a-sailing on the sea,' Hunter murmured.

'Four-and-twenty sailors stood between the masts,' Oupie countered, and Gia's mouth dropped open in a silent cry of shock.

'Did they really?' Hunter continued.

'No. Not really.'

'How many, then?'

'You tell me,' Oupie replied.

'Twelve at first but alas, only one set foot ashore.'

'Hunter Scott?' The men shook hands.

'I'm pleased to meet you,' Hunter murmured and stepped forward. He whispered something into Oupie's ear with a troubled look.

Oupie nodded ever so subtly. His chest heaved. Drawing Gia closer, he snuggled her into the circle of forearms. 'I assume that you've met Hunter?'

Hunter dipped his head in greeting. 'I work for the Countess of Stafford. She sent me to help, which is why Elias let me in here.'

And because it seemed safe to assume that Hunter meant no harm, Gia fastened an arm around Oupie's shoulders, slipped her fingers into his sandpaper palm and slid onto his lap. Everything about Oupie felt like home: the subtle scent of the sea, the reassuring reek of tobacco, but most of all, the child-like smug little purr that grumbled in his chest while she nuzzled her head into the crook of his neck.

Suddenly her insides were quarrelling, and she flooded with a rush of shame. Here she was, settling into heaven while Vuyo was missing. 'Vuyo!' Gia darted upright.

'Hush,' Oupie murmured.

'We have to find him!'

'And we will. There's something you need to know first. It can't wait.'

Gia shivered at the troubled gaze Oupie shared with Hunter.

'We thought you were dead,' Hunter accused, stooping to retrieve the scroll

'Mmm. Buried. It's a messy business.' Oupie blew his nose and followed it up with a vibrating snort that pulled up his wrinkled cheeks. He cupped Gia's chin in his palm and one side of his mouth curled upwards before he hugged her again. 'I assume that you know about the Finders Keepers claim by now?'

She nodded.

'Within days of the Sanderson brothers' debacle, I was being watched. I couldn't get my head around it because… if it was the guns or cargo from the *Velox* that someone wanted, why not confront me? I mean, I'm a wobbly old man who can't put up much of a fight.' Oupie gazed across False Bay, bits of his beard swaying in the breeze. 'When *they* accosted me finally, the fellow rambled on and on about an ancient scroll.' Oupie shrugged. 'So I did the only thing I could think of to protect everyone.'

'You hid?' Gia tested.

'No! *That* was accidental. I called Lady Stafford and gave her a piece of my mind because I got thinking; it's one thing tracing guns that have a ship's number intact. And even if a judge had sealed all the records of Pop's claim, there'd be ways and means around that. But for someone to know that an ancient scroll was aboard that ship and know it hadn't been returned to its rightful owner.' Oupie raised an imperious eyebrow. 'That kind of insight implied a direct link to the Earl's family.'

'What did Lady Stafford say?' Gia pried.

'That she had an inkling someone sabotaged the Velox. And she wanted the scroll, to see for herself if her niece was involved. She told me not to trust anyone other than Hunter Scott, and she gave me that rhyme. I panicked, though. The more I thought about it, the more I puzzled over why she believed a scroll would help her see things clearer. So I reckoned I'd take a look at it.' Oupie bobbed his head. 'Something I hadn't done before because Pop told me it was a blank parchment.'

'What happened?'

'I dodged a blade and found the cellar.'

'You mean dungeon?'

'It's a wine cellar. Then I remembered that Pop was attacked while being down there. He left home shortly after that. When I opened the scroll while I was down there, it exposed Pop's journal and I understood just how much trouble we were in.'

'Because the people who were after you didn't want Lady Stafford thinking that her granddaughter might have survived?' Gia frowned.

'Oh, Sweetheart.' Oupie's shoulders sagged. 'Haven't you figured it out yet? Lady Stafford's granddaughter isn't alive, she's dead.'

'How do you know?'

'Because I married her.'

Gia's heartbeat stuttered and Oupie's photo album flashed before her eyes. 'I'm related to Lady Stafford? That's why the girl on the cliff looked so familiar. Because of the newspaper article of Oumie in your photo album. It was her they found on a beach near here.'

Hunter smiled a bemused smile. 'Imagine my surprise that day I bumped into you and realised that the fate of the *Velox* was but one of our worries. The resemblance is uncanny. Grace had her grandmother's eyes and you have Grace's eyes. So, really, you have Lady Stafford's eyes.'

'That's how I got myself stuck in the scroll.' Oupie stretched his eyes. 'I already knew where the *Velox* lay, and while reading Pop's journal, I realised that your grandmother was found mere metres from its ultimate resting place. And around the same period as its disappearance. I thought if I came down here, I'd be able to see the crash and confirm my suspicion. But all I saw was Pop finding the *Velox* or retrieving its cargo. But stupid me touched him and got myself stuck. It wasn't until you opened the scroll earlier and we saw your grandmother crawling from that ship that I understood it only shows you memories of those related to you by blood.'

'And that will be proof enough for Lady Stafford,' Hunter added.

Gia blinked. It was a lot to absorb.

'Destroy it. Burn the scroll, Gia. Don't wait! If her niece gets her hand on it, she'll come for you.' Oupie gave her a long hug. 'Take her! Protect her! Make sure she knows who she can trust,' he told Hunter.

Gia whipped up onto her moonboot. 'What are you talking about? I'm not going anywhere without you, or Vuyo.'

Oupie came to his feet, sagging in the middle like a night time flower. He hobbled towards the edge of the cliff, staring across the bay as if seeing Table Mountain for the first time. Then he turned towards Gia slowly. 'I've lived a full life. A happy one. It wasn't always a perfect journey, but life never is, not for anyone. I've been luckier than most. For that I'm grateful. The only thing I'd change is…' Oupie's voice broke and little puddles of pain gathered in the corners of his eyes. 'I'd give anything for your mother to see how awesome her daughter has become. I love you, Sweetheart. Since you were brand new. No grandfather has ever been prouder.'

Gia's vision went blurry, her face got hot. Oupie's speech seemed bizarre. 'What are you… I don't understand… Why does it sound as if you're saying goodbye?'

Hunter came up behind her.

'A life for a life, Sweetheart, that's how the scroll seems to work. It's Vuyo's turn to live his life to the full. Give my godson my regards, will you? Tell him to help you celebrate my life. Tell everyone.' Oupie smiled, peaceful like, and opened the scroll.

Hunter scooped her up, throwing his arm around her waist. She reacted like a street cat: thrashing, punching, hissing. Vuyo's shouting ground Gia's outburst to a halt. She turned to look.

'She's too close to the edge!' Vuyo began running. He darted past a girl — a carbon copy of Gia — sprinting to help Grace.

'Vuyo! Don't! She isn't real!' Gia's replica called.

Grace looked up and in the split-second that her gaze met Vuyo's, she slipped.

'Grab my hand!' Vuyo lunged forward.

'Vuyo!' Gia's lookalike screamed.

'Quickly! Grab it!' Vuyo screamed at Grace. He slithered over the rock on his belly, focused. A second wave broke, bigger, more powerful. It crashed onto his back.

It's then that Oupie stepped forward and tugged Vuyo by the back of his rain jacket.

For a moment, everything was frozen in time.

'No. No!' Gia burst forward. A horrible fear gripped her heart when she realised the sacrifice Oupie intended making. This time forever. Hunter pulled her back, and she turned, drumming her fists against his chest as the woozy stirrings of panic overcame her.

A blinding bolt of light flashed.
The scroll fell to the ground.
When the light cleared, Gia's beloved Oupie was gone.

Chapter 22:

The bridge

Gia sat on her couch watching the approaching dusk cast tangerine streaks across a darkening sky. Shadows moved around her room as if reaching out to greet her. She ran her fingertips through the fur on Jinja's belly. Time and again; she glared at the door. Her dad had knocked three times already. She couldn't open it, she dared not. He'd see the pink, puffy eyes that looked back at her from the mirror.

The right thing to do was tell him everything; about the key, the riddle, the plateau, even their trip to the library and the man at the craft market. And yet, she couldn't help recall how he'd shunned her memory of Oupie surviving the car crash. It's how she knew he wouldn't believe a word of a tale that involved them finding Oupie with the help of an enchanted scroll and then losing him again. Not in a thousand lifetimes. But she couldn't blame him for not taking her word for things and then lie to him the moment it suited her, either. It would make her a… what did people call it? A hyper… hippo… hypocrite?

Then, of course, there was the matter of Tammy. She'd yanked open the door even before they'd reached the house. 'Look how honoured we are, our conquering hero's return,' she'd screeched, gripped them by their earlobes and tugged them across the threshold.

If it hadn't been for Hunter, their survival would have been a roll of the dice, at best. Gia didn't know what he'd said, only that the house had collapsed into a graveyard silence from which it hadn't yet recovered. Point being, she'd reached the safety of her bedroom without further rumblings. Which didn't excuse her behaviour or mean that she wouldn't have to apologise.

Gia showered, scrubbed her face until it was prawn-pink, then dressed in her red slacks that had white polka dots on them. She added a blue, fluffy pullover and yellow socks with paw-like soles on their bottoms. Then she packed her moonboot in the corner to dry and shoved the scroll into her pocket. She had no intention of burning it. Ever. Say now there was still a way to save Oupie? What then? And if she couldn't, what harm was there in looking at him through a vision from time to time. She'd put in the cellar. If it wasn't in the desk who would find it? Gia whirled to face the door. A minute later she was back on the couch. A minute after that, staring at the door again.

You can do it. You can! Gia reprimanded herself. She pulled her back straight, flung open the door, marched into the passage and found Vuyo sitting on the floor, looking downtrodden.

'I'm so sorry about what happened, Gia.'

'It isn't your fault. You know Oupie would do anything for us.' Gia made an effort to keep her voice even. She tried her utmost to be brave. The last thing she wanted Vuyo to do was play the blame game. Truth was, she wouldn't have been able to choose between him and Oupie.

Oupie knew that.

'He shouldn't have done this.' A frown played across Vuyo's forehead and his voice was thick with misery. 'Did *you* guess that Oupie had married Lady Stafford's granddaughter?'

'No. It's one helluva coincidence, though, don't you think? I wonder how they met?'

'She knocked on his door, that's how. My dad said that once Grace turned nineteen, she wanted to visit the shore where she'd been found. She hoped that it would jog her memory about her parents, where she'd come from, that sort of thing. But it's a ten-k walk unless you come across the sea. And she was afraid of water. You know that. So she stopped to ask if she could cut across Polymead Grove. It was love at first sight.' Vuyo held out a hand for her to pull him up with.

'Really?'

'That's what my dad said. He also said-'

'That I sent you the key.' Elias stepped into the corridor. 'But for no reason other than that it was a standing agreement with Samuel.' Elias held out his arms and Gia limped into them, hugging him as tightly as she could. 'If he'd still been here, we would have told you about the plateau on your sixteenth birthday. I wanted to tell you the moment he vanished, but...' Elias heaved a sigh. 'I suspected police would come, and I thought it best not to put you in a position where you'd have to lie to them.'

By the time Gia hobbled into the living room, Bongi was nursing a glass of sherry, Tammy perched on the couch and Elias moved around her, jingling ice into a cognac. As if puppets on the same string, everyone turned towards her. Tammy's eyes widened. She half-jumped across the room, scooping Gia into her arms, causing a painful knot in her chest. But the hardest part was figuring out who was consoling whom.

Gia became aware of her dad sitting at the piano, watching her. On the face of it, he appeared exhausted but relaxed. Their eyes met. All she saw was sorrow, and she wondered for a second if Hunter's tale hadn't perhaps broken him again. Did that mean her dad believed it, though?

He patted the piano seat beside him.

Gia shook her head.

Her dad held out an arm, curling his fingers into little hooks.

'It's time, Chile,' Bongi purred and Gia pondered, not for the first time, how she always seemed to know what was happening around her.

'I don't want to.' Gia opted to watch Elias throw back his head and down his cognac. A tear slipped down her cheek and she gave it a brisk wipe.

'Samuel's is not a life we mourn. No,' Bongi coaxed.

'Come, Sweetheart,' her dad whispered, his arm still extended. 'It doesn't help foraging around for a bunch of deep, dark reasons questioning why things happen a certain way. We've spent four months doing that and look where it got us. Not everything happens for a reason, they just happen because they happen. So maybe we should just play because we play.'

Gia's stomach twisted and Vuyo squeezed her hand. She took a tentative step forward. Short of throwing a tantrum, she couldn't see a way out. She sat, breathing deeply. Her dad hugged her and kissed the top of her head before tapping the left-most key. Keeping his hand slack, he ran it along the keyboard in a suave, zippy motion as if playing one long note. Gia placed her finger on the right-most key and imitated the movement.

A small smile crept to her dad's lips and his eyes seemed to sparkle with pleasure. Behind them, Tammy whimpered. Gia's dad played a series of random notes and each time she copied, shutting her eyes and breathing deeply on purpose, engrossed, almost without knowing. With each stroke, more and more warmth returned to the world.

Rat-a-tat! Someone rapped on the door.

'Elias!' It was Hunter.

'What?' Elias grunted, sounding annoyed.

'Fire!' Bongi breathed.

Gia gasped and her heart jumped. It was a word that people living on a farm never wanted to hear.

'In the fields?' Elias looked as if they had spanked him with a plank. 'But they're soaked?'

'The barn.'

Elias dropped his glass and began running. Gia's dad took off after him. Hunter lifted two fingers, pointing them at the guards on the terrace. The pair of them launched into a sprint and in a snap, Gia clicked that they worked for him.

Her first instinct was to help, but when she rushed onto the terrace, Hunter seized her elbow. 'Don't! This doesn't feel right.'

'I agree,' Vuyo nodded. 'Maybe a fire's just a fire, but what if it's not?'

'Is there a fire alarm?' Hunter asked.

Vuyo pointed at a red box mounted on the wall at the far end of the terrace. Hunter smashed the glass, pulled the lever. A siren sounded, rising to a crescendo. Sprinklers popped up, their sharp hiss of water resembling an angry den of snakes.

Gia watched their barn transform into long, licking stripes of orange, some of which reached roof height. In places, spurred on by a gusting wind, flames appeared to jump. She'd known from before she'd started school that panicked animals were impossible to control, they could merely be directed. One thing was sure, a stampede there would be. The best thing to do — the only thing — was stay out of their way. A nagging sense pricked that odd place between her shoulder blades. How did the fire get so big so fast? Could Hunter be right?

Elias opened the gates of the cow pen and cows crashed into each other, trampling in all directions. In the nick of time, because the roof collapsed. The sudden influx of oxygen spurred on the blaze. Planks exploded sideways, others leapt into the trees cracking branches. They dropped onto the lawn and sparks sprinted away in two neat-as-pin little rows.

Gia grasped the abnormality of that. Someone had doused it with something.

Flames scurried across the field. Straight through the fence, heading for the house.

One thing stood in their way.

'Lipica!' Gia broke into a sprint.

'Gia!' Vuyo screamed.

'No!' Hunter called.

Gia kept going. No way would she let Lipica burn alive. Not even *she* deserved that. Less than half-way across the lawn, the heat became an intense blur of warm fog. She tried not to think, not to feel, but her throat and nose burned, and her eyes wouldn't stop watering. She reached the paddock and used it to guide herself towards the latch.

Click! Gia flipped it.

Smack! Lipica rammed the gate.

It banged her chest and Gia dropped to the ground.

A panicked cow clipped her shoulder. She flinched as a hoof narrowly missed her fingers. She knew better than to stay down. Gia scrambled to her feet, but she'd lost her sense of direction. 'Help!' She spun round and round, searching for a reference point.

Someone fired a flare.

It ripped skyward.

Red.

Sizzling.

Hot.

It would be just like Vuyo to think of something as genius as that, and he'd know from their recent search of the study where Oupie kept them, Gia decided. She limped towards the spot where she thought the flare had originated. 'Vuyo?'

'Gia?'

'Vuyo!'

'Gia!' Vuyo's voice moved closer.

Footsteps approached.

A hulking, ash-covered figure in a patched cap came from nowhere. A blurry hand grabbed Gia's sweater and despite the heat, a blast of ice exploded down her spine. She pulled her sweater over her head, twisting out of it and sprinting away. But just like in a nightmare, her legs were slow. Unresponsive.

Vuyo charged after her, chocolate hair grey from ash. 'Yaah!' He slapped the hide of a disoriented cow before snatching Gia's hand and leading her across the cattle-grid.

'Stop! Don't move! Don't you dare move!' The fellow in the patched cap appeared beside them.

At close range, Gia thought his eyes wore that shrill, demented look of someone who belonged in an asylum.

'Get away from her!' Vuyo amazed Gia by lifting the flare gun. He wasn't pointing his shaky arm upwards, though. He aimed it at Mister Patchcap's chest. The fellow barged him to the ground. They rolled along the road towards the bridge. When they stopped, the flare gun was aimed at Vuyo's face.

'Don't!' Gia shrieked. Her mind ticked over. She searched for a weapon, a rock, plank, anything. Didn't find one. Only one option sprang to mind.

She pulled the scroll from her pocket and opened it.

Smoke cleared. Dusk snapped into the darkness of night. A car approached, and they whirled towards the oncoming sound. Oupie's sports car crossed onto the far end of the bridge. A large metal drum rolled into the road. The car veered left, skidding. There was a piercing screech as it hit the barrier, scraping against it, shooting up sparks.

Mister Patchcap darted from its path.

'Run!' Vuyo yelled, racing back towards her. His sharp black eyes met hers and Gia grasped the reality of the vision they were in just as Vuyo threw his arm around her waist, urging her into a limp-sprint. In his panicky haste, they banged against the barrier.

'Ouch!' Vuyo hollered and Gia caught the distinct sound of bone snapping as he groped for his elbow, bumping the scroll, causing her to drop it.

Nighttime evaporated.

Swirling smoke reappeared. It was dusk once more. Gia frisked the scroll from the ground and risked glancing around. She caught sight of a burly figure in a cap lumbering towards them.

'Open it! Open the scroll!' Vuyo shrieked. 'It's saving us. And it's showing us what happened on the bridge that day. We should have thought of it before.'

'Give me that thing!' Mister Patchcap hissed with such venom that Gia fumbled and fumbled and almost dropped the scroll again.

She hastened to unroll it, struggling with shaky fingers, and flinched at the sound of metal grinding on stone. Dusk had become night and Oupie's car could once again be seen casting sparks along the cement barrier of the bridge. It hit the metal drum and flipped, three, four times.

Mister Patchcap ducked, slamming into the barrier. He fell, clutching his ribs, looking dazed.

For a sickening second, the rolling vehicle sucked Gia's body towards it. It landed, lolling on its spine like a flipped over toad. *Whap, whap, whap,* its wheels spun close to their heads with its boot hanging over the edge of the cliff just past the bridge.

From the far side of the road, a small, skinny figure with a thatch of fair hair dashed towards the upside-down vehicle. 'Samuel! Are you alright? Do you need any help?'

Gia watched in horror as another version of Mister Patchcap appeared in the scroll's vision. He sprinted towards the skinny figure.

There was a bit of a dust-up.

'That's the man who's attacking us now!' Vuyo declared, pointing an accusatory finger. 'Which means, the small guy must be Deon Sanderson.'

The men carried on punching and kicking each other.

Behind them, the car's lights still lit the road and because of it, Gia witnessed the front windscreen of Oupie's sports car pop out. Oupie hauled himself through the gap wearing red trainers and a blood-soaked shirt. He heaved, pulling Gia's lookalike from the vehicle.

Oupie picked her lookalike up, raced into the field and ducked below a canopy of leaves, milliseconds before Deon Sanderson held up his hands in a gesture of surrender. Mister Patchcap's lookalike ignored him. He grabbed Deon Sanderson by the chest and lugged him towards the upside vehicle, wrestling him into it.

It was the same moment that Hunter sprinted from the swirl of smoke into the clarity of their vision. Like a lamb from a lion, the real Mister Patchcap tried darting away, but Gia's dad appeared, and then Elias.

Gia closed the scroll.

She didn't have the heart to watch Oupie's car fall into the gorge.

Chapter 23:

Lady Stafford

'Are you sure about this, Dad?' Gia frowned. 'It feels like bragging.'

'We're welcoming her, showing her who we are. How can it be bragging?'

'Here she comes!' Vuyo chimed from his lookout post at the window and as if the piano stool didn't already have an excellent view of the driveway.

They watched a grand old lady clothed in a frothy lace top emerge from a black vehicle.

Hunter bowed, pecked her hand and offered her his elbow. Her ring — was it a wedding ring? — twinkled, as did her enormous blue eyes. A small smile played on Gia's lips because they were identical to her own, just like Hunter said.

Lady Stafford was rosy-cheeked, petite, with painted nails and bundles of wrinkles on her face. She appeared fragile, but it wasn't weighing her down. Her shoulders hunched and her neck was perhaps too frail for the string of gemstones draped around it. Gia speculated how it felt being so old. Was it sore? It had to be strange watching the world change. Tammy said that in Lady Stafford's youth there weren't computers or cellphones and not everyone had indoor plumbing. *Imagine that!* What Gia didn't have to imagine was that Lady Stafford wore slacks.

'Ready?' Gia's dad nudged her. 'On three. One. Two. Three.'

Gia began softly, coaxing their chosen duet from the keys. Her fingers flew over them and as always, her dad pressed the pedals, teasing a deep pitter-patter from the lower end of the bass. Before Gia realised, the music engrossed her.

Lady Stafford had settled on their couch by the time they turned to face the room. She'd kicked off her shoes and swayed to the music. Gia walked towards her and curtsied, trying not to grin.

Lady Stafford beamed and beckoned with cocked fingers and Gia got the subtle sense of someone who was used to being obeyed. 'Thank you. My son played, you know.'

'My dad taught me.' Gia pulled at her scratchy skirt and curtsied again.

'I hate them, don't you?' Lady Stafford confided.

'Tammy made me wear it.' Gia jumped on the bandwagon, shooting Tammy a demure glance. 'She says that I should try to be more flexible and change the way I do things sometimes.'

'I see.' Lady Stafford nodded, eyes wise as those of an ancient tortoise. 'Well, to be fair, a wise woman once said that without change there wouldn't be butterflies.' Her eyes flitted over Gia's bracelet, becoming moist. Rolling back the sleeve of her top, she lifted her wrist.

Lady Stafford's bracelet matched. 'It was my son's parting gift, a way of ensuring that Grace and I would be forever united.'

The rest of the day passed like a dream.

Lady Stafford kissed Jinja on the head. She apologised to Nina for Hunter's unfortunate behaviour and lingered at Lipica's side for an eternity. 'Lipizzaners are majestic creatures,' she murmured, stroking Lipica's mane and hugging her time and again. She pulled on a pair of Gia's gumboots and wobbled through the cowshed, pulling a bunch of faces and leaning heavily on Vuyo's shoulder while he protected the plaster cast on his arm. Though he seemed quite proud of it, Gia thought.

Detective Steele joined them for a lunch of Tammy's traditional Bobotie. 'Sign here, please.' He ordered and placed Oupie's guns back on the desk. He turned to Lady Stafford and bobbed his head. 'Thank you for the gun licences. I've just spoken to someone from Interpol.'

'That's the international police,' Vuyo whispered into Gia's earlobe.

'The fellow Hunter captured on the bridge has agreed to testify, and so has the man from the craft market,' Detective Steele said.

'Against my niece?'

'I'm afraid so. They arrested her a few moments ago.'

***

'Bye! I'll come again!' Tito, their friend from the ice cream parlour, yelled and Vuyo waved at the departing vehicle.

Gia flicked river water at Jinja's nose. She nipped happily at the droplets before growing bored with the game and falling onto her stomach across a blowup mattress, legs stretched back as if she was double-jointed. Nina kept a sturdy-eye on Hunter, who was brushing his teeth down by the river.

The kettle on their camp stove whistled. Gia poured three steaming cups and kicked Vuyo's ankle that poked from the door of his tent.

'I overhead my mom talk about buying you more dresses,' Vuyo confided, stifling a yawn.

'I'm not wearing them.'

'I've asked her to get me a lah-di-dah coat, so you can call me lord if you want to.'

'Stop it.'

'You're going to have to watch your tone now that you're going to be a lady. Will you be Lady Stafford the third or Lady Lance the first, do you think?'

Gia shot him a look that she thought would sink a submarine before turning towards the approaching drone of an engine and galloping of hooves.

'Whoa!' Her dad pulled Lipica's reigns. He leaned over her mane, stroking her neck before hopping off and allowing her to amble under the trees. 'I hope there's enough food. I'm famished.'

Elias pulled the car into the shade and the entire family climbed out: Tammy, Bongi and Lady Stafford. Vuyo rushed to help her quiver her way down to Oumie's bench that watched over the river while Gia's dad steered Bongi by her elbow.

Gia scurried to hug them.

'I brought you something.' Lady Stafford handed Gia a photo in a frame.

150

'Was that you?' Vuyo asked 'Wow! Hunter wasn't kidding, you looked just like Gia.'

'Young man, I look nothing like Gia.' Lady Stafford waggled a wrinkled finger. 'But every bit of Gia looks something like me.'

Gia giggled at the delicious reprimand and began helping Tammy lay a table with breakfast goodies. They feasted on figs, cheese, honey, pickled ginger, boiled eggs and toast with spicy mince.

Lady Stafford smacked her dainty lips and while Gia cleared plates away, she got serious. 'I'm afraid that it's time to bid farewell.'

'Already? It's only been a week. Did my dad find the Earl's grave? Are you taking him back to Scotland?' It surprised Gia to find that she didn't want Lady Stafford to leave. She was just getting used to having her Great-Great Grandmother around, and she cherished it.

'Yes, yes, and no.' Lady Stafford eyed the waterfall. 'Your father is going to put him next to Grace. I'm sure my son would prefer that. It makes little sense for me to separate him from his daughter. And I can't very well take Grace. It would be cruel to move her from the burial ground of a family she knew and loved into the burial ground of a family she'd forgotten, don't you think? I do. She should stay where she is. That way they can lay your grandfather to rest beside her.'

'That won't be possible, not anymore,' Gia murmured and caught Elias eyeing her sheepishly.

The grand old woman waved Vuyo closer and took Gia's hand. 'I've been thinking. I'd be much obliged if the pair of you would consider doing me a kindness.'

'Of course. Anything.' Gia jumped at the opportunity.

'I want to trade places with Samuel.'

Gia sat, more like fell, onto the bench beside her.

'Now, now. Come! No crying. It's cause for celebration.' Lady Stafford brushed a tear from Gia's cheeks and ran her finger across Gia's bracelet. 'We're joined forever through these, you and me. Nothing can ever change that.'

Gia sniffled.

'Please, Chile,' Lady Stafford looked across at Bongi and smiled. Both Tammy and Bongi chuckled. 'I've spent more than half my life searching for my son and Grace. Sometimes it feels as if it's what I was born to do.' She took Vuyo's hand. 'And now that I've found them… well… didn't you say that while the scroll trapped you in that vision, you spoke to Grace? Touched her?'

Vuyo nodded, dabbing his eyes with a roll of his shoulder.

'And she spoke back?'

Another nod.

'I don't have much time left, a couple of weeks. Months if I'm lucky.' Lady Stafford dropped both her voice and her chin, staring up at them. 'The last time I was ill, my physician called the priest. I'm not kidding. There's no cure for old-age, you understand, don't you?'

'It will be uncomfortable there,' Gia murmured, unsure of what to do about the suggestion that she both loved and hated.

'No. Elias has packed a crate with tents, mattresses and food galore. We'll tie it to my ankle so I can take it with and before I touch your grandfather, Elias will help me throw a rope down to my son. I'll get him to erect the tent.'

Gia didn't know what to say. Was it so awful to want Oupie and Lady Stafford to be with her? After a long moment, she murmured, 'As long we're forced to sacrifice someone we love into the scroll, its curse isn't broken.'

'It is what it is.'

'But what if you could be with them and with us?'

'Accept the things you cannot change, Chile,' Bongi murmured.

'Do you think the scroll minds what kind of life is used to break the curse?'

Lady Stafford tilted her head to the side.

'What if… after you've been in the scroll for a week or so and spent time with everyone, we tried to bring you back by sending in a butterfly?'

'Why a butterfly?'

'No reason, other than.' Gia shrugged. 'They don't seem to mind change, they're always content and they're the closest thing to magic of anything I can think of. I doubt they care which era they live in.'

'Well, what have we got to lose,' Lady Stafford smiled.

***

Oupie came whirling into the kitchen singing one of his fabulous false tunes.

'Unbelievable! Here you are, acting as if nothing happened when all that time I spent crying I could have been making jam!' Tammy shrieked for the fourth time in as many weeks.

'Only the good die young, you should have known better!' Oupie wrapped his arms around Tammy's neck and smacked a kiss onto her cheek before puffing on his pipe, looking unreasonably pleased. In the background, Bongi gave a throaty chuckle.

Gia hastily threw together a pile of picnic food. Oupie poured himself a cup of tea, whipped up his morning eggs and they fell into step beside him, making their way to his favourite bench.

'We're going to swing by the graveyard and then head for the river. Vuyo's going to teach me to swim,' Gia chattered, patting the towel she'd draped across her shoulders while Oupie positioned himself towards the sunrise.

'And then we're going to look for what Pop found in those crates. Treasure, I assume. So if you know something…' Vuyo hunched forward, licking his lips in optimistic anticipation.

Oupie snorted, he looked momentarily confused before shifting his pipe into the corner of his lips. 'Did his journal mention finding treasure?'

'Not exactly, no.' Vuyo pulled his back straight.

'Did I?'

'Fun fact, Pop mention finding secret compartments in those crates,' Vuyo quipped.

'Point being, that doesn't mean there was anything in them.'

'Do you honestly think that Pop would have claimed the *Velox* if there wasn't?' Vuyo said, a bit rudely, Gia thought. 'I suppose you also think that Pop would have handed over its coordinates if he'd lost the case?'

'I don't know what Pop should have, could have, might have, would have done.' Oupie threw up an arm as if mortified that Vuyo would propose he spend his time considering something with such dubious merits. 'Pop won. The judge said so! Nothing else matters. Now off with you. I want to eat my eggs in peace.'

Gia picked some flowers and began skipping towards the cattle-grid. No moonboot, no problem.

'By the way,' Oupie yelled to their backs. 'Tell Tammy that I need to show you the ways of Apiarists. She can build it into your extra-mural schedule.'

Gia spun so fast, she tripped over herself and Oupie dissolved into a fit of chuckles. All his wrinkles creased inwards as if tugged by secret strings. 'I don't want to be an Apiarist!'

'Me neither, I'm scared of bees!' Vuyo hollered.

Oupie lifted a furry eyebrow. 'Since when? They're harmless.'

'No, they aren't. Have you seen the way they act if you drop a hive? Even in the rain?' Vuyo complained.

Oupie's eyes narrowed. He placed his plate of eggs on the bench and came to his feet. 'You dropped one of my hives?' he slurred in a tone that had undergone a radical transformation.

'We were trying to get away from Hunter. It was before we knew that he worked for Lady Stafford. It wasn't our fault.' Vuyo backtracked.

'What was the number on the box?' Oupie took a step towards them. He removed his pipe from his mouth and blew away the smoke.

Gia blinked. The question seemed cryptic.

'The number, Gia?'

'I never looked at the box.'

'Me neither, I was running for my life,' Vuyo concurred.

'Fetch it,' Oupie commanded.

'The fallen hive? I'm not going back there. Just now they remember me,' Gia said with a scrunched up nose and petrified croak.

'They will. Bees have long memories, they must have if they fly such distances without getting lost. For all we know, that little colony's plotting revenge.' Vuyo decided.

'Listen to me carefully, both of you. You mentioned that it was raining. And cold, wet bees are dead bees. Those little souls are endangered. Didn't Tammy teach you that? You should be ashamed of yourselves for wiping out an entire village just so you could save your bacon.'

Gia's jaw dropped. There was little doubt Oupie was unamused. Even so, there was something in his voice, something about his request, and something about the way his manner pricked that spot between her shoulder blades.

'I want that hive, Gia,' Oupie declared. 'Today! You can learn to swim tomorrow. We need to see what we can salvage.'

Gia glared at him in disbelief. Vuyo kicked a stone across the grass.

'The queen could still be alive. Maybe she can regrow the colony,' Oupie moaned.

'Fine! But I'm not bringing her if she's grumpy,' Gia moaned.

'Fine!' Oupie imitated Gia's manner to the tee.

She giggled and sprinted back towards him, hugging him around his belly. 'Missed you.'

'Missed you more.' Oupie grinned.

Vuyo grumbled his frustration all the way to the graveyard, muttering and kicking stones with his heel, hands deep in his pockets.

Gia placed flowers in front of her mom's grave, then Oumie's, before moving towards a newly erected headstone. It read:

Annamay Gracelyn Stafford,
2nd Countess of Stafford,
Beloved Mother, Grandmother,
Great grandmother, Great-Great Grandmother and dearest friend.

'I'm glad she could spend some time with the Earl and with Grace,' Vuyo smiled a sad smile.

'Me too. But I'm glad we got her out of the scroll and got to show her our home movies before she died.'

'She liked that.'

Gia nodded, wiping a tear. 'Now everyone's together just like they should be.'

'Come!' Vuyo took her by the hand. 'Let's not be sad. She didn't want that.'

They charged down to the river with a hot wind on their backs.

'There!' Gia pointed at the hive that was mushed in parts, buried beneath layers of the broken box and caked with a deposit of mud. It lay against the tree at an odd angle.

They approached with the stealth of cats.

'It's number twenty.' Vuyo pointed at the lid, dug his hand into the mud. 'And look, here's the riddle. I must have dropped it that day we were trying to escape.'

'That's one of the hives that would have gone to your dad if we hadn't found Oupie.' Gia poked it with a random stick and scrambling for cover, leaving Vuyo to fend for himself.

Nothing came out.

They crawled closer.

Vuyo lifted the lid with Gia's stick as tentatively as if it were a scorpion's tail.

Still nothing.

'Oupie's going to be so mad,' Gia murmured.

Vuyo shoved the stick through the hive's rope handles. An odd jingle-jangle sound came from inside.

They took a collective breath, eyes snapping wide. Gia removed the lid and peered at the little hexagon shapes that made up a honeycomb, aptly matching the symbol of Polymead Grove's logo. She looked at Vuyo and smiled that stupid cat smile people got when they knew something they weren't supposed to.

'No way.' Vuyo threw himself onto the ground and turned the hive upside-down. Out tumbled a yellow velvet bag, no bigger than his hand. Vuyo opened its neck and emptied a trio of sparkling diamonds into his palm.

Gia threw the back of her hand across her gaping mouth.

'Told you there was treasure.' Vuyo stretched his all-knowing eyes. 'What are we going to do with it?'

Those who know thereof do not speak.

'That's because they can't. They're bees.' Vuyo grinned in admiration.

'They aren't all bees. Oupie knew the risk he was taking when he sent us here, but he took it anyway. These diamonds are the reason only he and your dad work with the hives. It must also be the reason he wants *us* to be Apiarists. So what do you say, Vuyo?'

'To what? Do I want to be an Apiarist?'

'Can you keep a secret?'

Vuyo's eyes flashed and his face cracked into a grin. 'I'm already keeping one.'

About the author

J.T. GROBLER lives with her husband and daughter in Somerset West, South Africa. She shares her space with two formidable, but kind souled, Staffordshire terriers – Misty Dusks Magical Gimli & Boldwin Lumos Nox.

When she isn't writing, she's probably strolling with her furry friends through the local farmer's vineyards or dawdling along the beach. She adores watching an active slipway. She also has a pair of African Grey parrots who love to jabber about what she said yesterday.

Her first writing job came from a third-grade teacher – 100 lines of *I must not eat in class.*

Acknowledgements

Where to start? Oh, my goodness!
Hats off to my daughter, for patiently bobbing through my endless prattling. Thanks to my super-duper husband, for gently accepting that today, like so many other days, would be a writing day. Selma Leach, I appreciate your genuine, ongoing interest and trusty council. An enormous bowl of thanks to Cecily van Straten. What a delightful mentor you are! Emily House — Wow! — talk about magic. A special acknowledgement also goes to my insightful writing group. Every comment is invaluable. And, of course, I better not forget. Thank you, Gimli and Nox! For snoring at my feet, hour after hour and creating that wonderfully furry and cosy environment every scribbler thrives on. And without which, I dare say, the entire experience would be left wanting.

www.ingramcontent.com/pod-product-compliance
Lightning Source LLC
Chambersburg PA
CBHW030748110726
47900CB00008B/2505